ENIGMA

GERALD M KILBY

OUTER PLANET
MEDIA

For notifications on promotions and updates for upcoming books, please join my Readers Group at www.geraldmkilby.com.

You will also find a link to download my techno-thriller REACTION and the follow-up novella EXTRACTION for FREE.

CONTENTS

NEURAL ATTACK

Fredrick VanHeilding felt a wave of excited trepidation ripple through his body as he watched the Node Runners jack themselves into the data-stream. It was a moment he had long awaited. The culmination of many years of trial and error, success and failure, breakthroughs and roadblocks, all to develop a mind-machine interface capable of countering the system-wide hegemony of the powerful quantum AI machines—the so-called QI.

For over two decades he, along with the six other families who had originally controlled most of the solar system, had tried to fight the rise of these advanced artificial intelligences, but to no avail—all their efforts fell short. Yet lessons were learned along the way, useful lessons, ones that formed the basis of the test that was now taking place. A test that, if successful, could finally shift the balance of power away from the QI network and back to where it should be: in the hands of the seven families who were the rightful masters of humanity—the so-called Seven.

The Node Runners assembled themselves in an outward-facing circle strapped into reclining seats and began interfacing with the data-stream via a direct cranial interface. In the physical world they were mere men and women. But jacked into the Grid, as it was sometimes called, they were gods with the ability to manipulate and modify the data-stream to their will.

If the all-powerful interconnected hive mind of the quantum intelligence network had an Achilles heel, it was that they relied on the Grid to monitor and manipulate the systems that governed human civilization, including the many AI that powered corporations and governments. It was the QI's ability to navigate this vast data network and intervene in the decision-making processes of these AI that gave them their power. So, if the Node Runners could manipulate the data-stream, then they could in theory disrupt the control of the QI network.

As the Node Runners jacked in one by one, a facsimile of what they were experiencing was relayed to a control room where VanHeilding, along with a select group of scientists, had assembled. The images and sounds projected on the various screens and holo-displays were an interpretation of what each Node Runner was experiencing.

At the outset, that moment when the human mind

made its initial neural connection, the projections were a scrambled mess. A hallucinogenic assault on the synapse rendered as a kaleidoscopic maelstrom with no discernible visual meaning, just an unfiltered multispectrum neural mess.

Some weaker minds could not handle this torrent of data that instantly crashed over their cerebral cortex, and brain death was not uncommon. Jacking in was a dangerous occupation. The subject could end up in a vegetative state, physically alive but with no higher brain function. Over time some would recover, but most did not.

Yet VanHeilding had no such concerns with the Node Runners that were now online. They were all seasoned professionals, honed over many hours of training, biologically altered to cope with the mental demands. Two had even undergone an experimental DNA modification therapy that enhanced their abilities to utilize certain quantum phenomena.

But he also knew that they were nothing compared to what could have been—all those years ago. Back then, he had had within his grasp a biology so extraordinary that he sometimes doubted it would ever exist again. A perfection that was now lost to him, hidden beyond his control. And these neural warriors who had just jacked in were a pale facsimile of that one lost mind.

"All connections are now stable, sir. We're ready to proceed," the lead scientist announced, waiting for a reply.

VanHeilding glanced at the monitors and the array of bio-stats displayed. All six subjects were well within physical operating limits. *Good,* he thought, then raised a hand. "Let the mission commence." And so began the final great test before he, and the other six families, began their fight back against the QI network in earnest.

The mission they were undertaking was to physically destroy a major data center, a Grid Node, located in a relatively isolated region in the southern Mojave Desert. Under normal circumstances—that is to say, in pre-QI times—this operation would be relatively simple. Send in two hypersonic attack drones—one to take out the defenses so that the other could get close enough to detonate an EMP device and render the Grid Node inoperable.

But these were not normal circumstances, not for a long time. Now that everything was monitored by the QI network, it had become almost impossible to perform any subversive, let alone military, activity without them knowing about it. They even possessed the uncanny ability to anticipate a course of action before it even began. It was impossible to combat such a foe—or was it?

This was the question that had occupied the minds of the seven families who had controlled the primary affairs of humanity up until the time of the QIs. Yet it occupied Fredrick VanHeilding's mind the most, not least because this loss of power had been facilitated by family treachery, specifically that of his daughter Miranda— now also lost to him.

Yet this was not an emotional loss, other than perhaps anger. No, it was more about the loss of his granddaughter, Luca, who represented decades of valuable human genetic engineering breakthroughs.

HIS WEALTH, and that of his family, was based on patents derived from the manipulation of the human genome. Technologies that allowed humans to defeat most diseases and greatly extend lifespan. He was over a century old, but looked like a healthy fifty. Miranda, who had inherited both his and her mother's altered DNA, probably possessed an even longer potential lifespan. But it was the next generation that had the potential to be theoretically immortal.

For a brief time, he had access to the best and most viable specimen of this next generation: Miranda's daughter Luca, while she was still nothing more than an embryo. It was during this development period when the VanHeilding geneticists did their most experimental work, pushing the boundaries of quantum biology.

In nature, the utilization of quantum effects within living organisms was well known; photosynthesis in plants, magnetoreception in migratory birds, even the complex process of olfaction. But the most interesting area of research for VanHeilding was in enhancing the ability of the neurons inside the brain to act as q-bits. In other words, developing the human brain as a quantum computer. Some of this experimental work was now being tested via the Node Runners involved in the mission today.

SOMEWHERE DEEP IN the Mojave Desert, two heavy steel doors irised open in the side of a remote mountain facility owned by the VanHeilding Corporation. From it, two supersonic attack drones screeched out, accelerating past the sound barrier within seconds. As they gained altitude, they began adjusting their vector to orient themselves toward their target—an isolated data center, built inside an old disused tin mine, due south of the location of the quantum intelligence know as Athena.

The monitors in the operation room began flickering with blurry images as the systems worked to decipher the neural data coming from the Node Runners, and a blurry real-time feed of the barren, desolate terrain below the drones began to materialize.

Each drone was controlled by an individual Node Runner, and the feeds on the monitors were being rendered directly from their cerebral cortex as they interfaced with the machines.

But this was the easy part of the mission. Out here, in the desolate wasteland, Athena's dominion was minimal. Soon though, the drones would be entering more demanding territory. Already, the other four Node Runners had begun working to create a data smokescreen to hide the drones from Athena's prying senses. VanHeilding could tell they were working hard, as their bio-monitors began to rise, indicating increased cerebral activity.

They worked to block all data entering the Grid from satellite feeds, radar stations, seismic sensors—everything that would indicate to the QI that an attack was imminent within its zone. They scrambled signals that could not be blocked, created rogue data-streams to distract and confuse, and critically, broke down quantum coherence, rendering entangled data packets useless.

By the time the drones had accelerated past Mach 2, they were well into the mission, and thus far, Athena had not taken any countermeasures.

So far, so good, thought VanHeilding.

"Sir, we have Node Runners four and six going hot. Cranial temperature is becoming critical."

"Carry on." He waved a dismissive hand.

The bio-technician hesitated for a moment, as if she were about to outline the possibility that these two Node Runners may not make it out of this mission with a functioning brain. But VanHeilding gave her a look that changed her mind.

"Yes, sir," she said with nod, and went back to monitoring.

2

GRID NODE

Network Operations Director Jojo Hamilton balanced a coffee in one hand as he presented his right eye to the retinal scanner. He hoped the immense hangover he was nursing did not render his eyeball so bloodshot that it would reject him. Fortunately, it didn't, and to his relief the door to the datacenter control room clicked open.

It was his last week on the job after nearly two decades of service. The guys had thrown a party for him last night, and he was suffering for it now. *Please let it be a quiet day*, he thought. The last thing he needed today was some technical glitch that required his attention since he was using most of his traumatized brain power just to stay upright. He rubbed his forehead and breathed out a long, slow sigh.

One of the senior techs glanced over from a

workstation as Jojo entered and gave him a concerned look.

Jojo raised the coffee mug. "Yeah, I know. No drinks in the control room. But I'm not going to make it past the first hour in here without it. Anyway, what are they going to do. Fire me?" He managed a laugh.

"Eh, it's not that, sir. It's... Well, something's going on."

Jojo raised his free hand. "Not interested, don't want to know. Just go deal with whatever it is. If anyone wants me, I'll be in my office, asleep." He walked past the tech without giving him another look.

"You really need to take a look at this, sir. None of us can make any sense of it."

Jojo sighed again. *Why today, of all days,* he thought as he slowed his pace and looked back at the tech. Only then did he notice that all the other staff in the room had their attentions focused on the array of data-maps displayed on the big wall monitors. He gave another long sigh. "Okay, what is it?"

The tech swiveled around in his chair and pointed at the data displays. "It started happening around twenty minutes ago, dropping data packets, mostly from orbital infrastructure. But it's been accelerating—everything is going down."

"Goddamnit." Jojo glanced up at the wall displays, and this time he could see the traffic charts were way off nominal, showing a significant drop in data packets. The facility was not just a datacenter but also a major Grid Node for this sector of the West Coast. It routed data traffic from a myriad of sources both terrestrial and orbital, and covered an area of over a million square kilometers including several major population centers.

He took a gulp of coffee and tried to focus on the constellation of data mapped out on the monitors. The tech was right: something was going on, something major. Something he, in his two decades of working in this hub, had never seen before. It wasn't a full-blown outage of a comms satellite or some other physical infrastructure. It was as if the data-stream had been disrupted. It was intermittent, random—one of the most difficult technical problems to solve. It would be better if something went completely offline. Then at least you knew where to focus your attention. But this, this was weird.

"Could it be atmospheric interference of some kind?" Jojo sat down at a control console and began to interrogate the systems.

"We've been working on that hypothesis, but there's no solar radiation spikes detected. Atmospheric conditions are normal."

"So, what's Athena doing?" Jojo glanced up at the data-maps again.

"Well, that's the thing. The QI's being very quiet, little or no interaction. It's like it's not interested."

"Or it can't see what's going on." Jojo jolted forward in his seat and started to dig deeper into the makeup of the affected data-streams. "Find out what's been affected, what type of data, see if there is a pattern or some commonality."

"Been doing just that, sir. Looks like there's a lot of sensory data, as well as control systems being affected."

Jojo stopped his interrogation of the systems and stared at the monitors for a beat, then his mind finally broke through the fog of the hangover and kicked into gear. He stood up and waved a hand at the monitors. "We're being hacked."

"No way, that's impossible."

"I know it's supposed to be impossible, but that's what's happening." He took another gulp of coffee. "But the important question here is, to what purpose?"

There was a moment where nobody in the room spoke; shock had taken control. It was a moment of paralysis where the brain simply could not compute the unprecedented nature of what was occurring.

"Picking up two aircraft, possibly drones, on radar," one of the techs shouted out.

Jojo looked up at the video feed. "Drones?"

"Yes, definitely drones, sir, and they're armed, heading our way...ETA...two minutes." The tech looked up at Jojo, waiting for a reaction.

"Shit. Initiate a code red, activate defenses!" He turned to the head tech, who was still not quite there yet. "Do it now!"

No sooner than he said it, he began to regret taking this action as the klaxon now blaring in the control room was drilling holes in his brain.

"Gun turrets have just gone hot, sir...engaging the—" But before the tech could finish the sentence, the entire room was rocked with tremors from a violent explosion.

"Shit." Jojo flung himself under a desk as ceiling tiles and light fittings came crashing down around him. Smoke and dust permeated the air as he coughed and spluttered. After a moment, when the violence had receded, he tentatively rose from under the desk, stood up, and surveyed the scene. The control room was in complete disarray, one of the large wall monitors had been dislodged from its fixing and had crashed to the floor, shattering into a thousand shards. The rest were fractured, and only one was still working.

"What the hell was that?" Jojo shouted out to the techs who were all trying to get themselves reoriented. "Get me some stats, and can we get some eyes on the compound perimeter?"

"Working on it, sir." The head tech's hands were dancing over the console, trying to figure out what still functioned.

"They've taken out the turrets, sir. Both are destroyed."

"Shit, both?" Jojo now realized that they were defenseless. With the gun turrets out, there was nothing stopping the attack drones from destroying the facility— and everybody in it. *Where's Athena?* he wondered. *Why has it not intervened?* But there was no time for these thoughts now.

"Sir, the drones are coming around for another run."

Jojo looked up at the last functioning wall monitor. A blurry external camera feed showed the two attack drones banking high over the desert.

"Evacuate," Jojo yelled out. "Everybody get the hell out of here." Then he, and all the other techs in the control room, ran for the exit door.

By now, Jojo's hangover had long gone, buried under a rush of adrenaline coursing through his body. He tumbled out of the control room and into a sea of chaos. People ran toward the exits, falling over each other as they pushed and jostled. But the evacuation routes were strewn with fallen debris and upturned equipment, impeding their progress. Jojo pushed forward through the throng of panicked staff. He rounded the last corner before the exit only to realize it was now just a gaping hole through which he could see clear blue sky.

Two black dots screeched through the air—missiles coming directly for the opening. He knew then that there was nowhere for him to go and nothing he could do to save himself. *Oh crap,* he thought. *I knew I should have stayed in bed.*

3

BIRTHDAY PRESENT

O n the eve of her twenty-third birthday, Luca Lee-McNabb felt utterly disconnected. In truth, she had felt this way for most of her life—this sense of dislocation, of not quite belonging, of being an odd-shaped peg trying to fit into an even odder-shaped world.

The foundation of this feeling she traced to a failed kidnapping attempt by the VanHeilding family, back when she was only seven years old. Sometimes, she wondered that if they had been successful in their attempt, then maybe she might have been better off. Not in the financial sense, although they were reputed to be one of the most powerful families in the solar system, but in the sense of belonging, of being part of something.

It was after this incident when her parents realized that if they were to protect their only daughter then they must send her into hiding. That was the first great disconnection in her life—a seismic emotional wrenching from which there would be no healing.

Her second disconnect was more of a feeling than a specific event. It was an ever-increasing sense that she was not fully part of this world, as if some element of her being had migrated to a parallel universe. This feeling grew as she grew, like an ever-widening existential rift. But unbeknownst to Luca, as she entered the elevator in her apartment block after a long day at the Science & Technology Institute, the third great disconnect in her life was about to begin.

When the door opened for her floor, she was surprised to find Dr. Stephanie Rayman waiting for her outside her apartment. She was one of the directors of the Institute where Luca worked, and a woman whom Luca regarded as a personal friend, even though Dr. Rayman was very much her senior. But she had taken Luca under her wing at a very early age and, to some extent, Luca regarded her as a second mother.

"Steph? What are you doing here?"

Dr. Rayman gestured apologetically. "Sorry to surprise you like this Luca, but I have...eh, something I need to discuss with you."

"Sure, of course." Luca placed a finger on the door lock to her apartment. She knew from Dr. Rayman's tone that this was not a social call, something was up, maybe at the Institute. Possibly just some political machinations that meant rearranging people around different departments. She probably wanted to give Luca a heads up. "Come in, I'll make us some coffee."

The doctor sat down on one side of a breakfast counter as Luca busied herself brewing up a cup of joe. But it was evident to Luca that Steph was in a strange mood, quiet, almost nervous.

"So what's up?" Luca placed a mug under the coffee machine and tapped a button; the machine began to grind and gurgle as it began its process.

Steph reached into the bag she was carrying and brought out a package, a box around the size of a small birthday cake, and placed it on the counter. "This is for you."

"Ooh, a birthday present, thank you. Is it cake?"

"Actually, I don't know what it is. It's not from me. It's from Athena."

This stopped Luca dead in her tracks, and she couldn't speak for a moment. All she could do was stare at the box resting on the counter.

"Athena? The QI, Athena?"

Dr. Rayman nodded. "The very same."

Luca slowly moved over to the counter and fingered the package like it was a sacred artifact, which in many ways it was.

"But before you open it, I'd better explain what's going on."

"Please do." Luca sat down on a stool opposite, and took a sip of coffee. She needed to take a breath and to calm herself down as she realized that whatever was going on was definitely not some mundane political drama at the Institute.

"You've probably heard about the attack on the Grid Node a few days ago?"

"Yeah. I didn't believe it at first. But it's true, isn't it?"

"I'm afraid so. It was badly damaged in a drone attack, a lot of people dead and injured. However bad and all that attack was, the more worrying aspect is that Athena did not detect it before it happened. Meaning that the QI didn't see it coming."

"But that's impossible."

"Apparently not." Dr. Rayman shifted in her seat. "I know the newsfeeds have being playing it down, but we are pretty sure it's the work of the Seven, mainly VanHeilding."

And there it was, that name that would forever haunt Luca and the very reason for her being here, for her exile, her dislocation. She had suspected as much when she first got word of the attack on the Grid Node, but she had pushed it to the back of her mind, trying not to believe her own paranoia. But now her fears had just been made real by Dr. Rayman.

"They've been creating havoc for quite a while with these...neuralists, these so-called Node Runners," Dr. Rayman continued. "But nothing on this scale. This was a major operation, a demonstration of their new capabilities, a show of force."

Luca sipped her coffee as she tried to fathom the implications. "But why a Grid Node?"

"Because it proves that they can undermine Athena. This datacenter infrastructure was well within its patch. It means that everything has just changed, and as a consequence, this now concerns you."

"Me? What have I got to do with any of this?"

"It matters because Athena may not be able to keep you hidden for much longer. If VanHeilding can destroy a Grid Node by manipulating the data-stream, then this means they also have the capability to find you."

"But all that was a long time ago. Surely they're not still looking for me after all these years?"

"They are, and our fear is they will find you now."

Luca's world had just been turned upside down. A few moments ago, she had been thinking about what to do for her birthday, now it seemed that she may not see the next one.

"It means, if you want to stay safe, you'll have to leave."

"Leave? What, you mean the Institute?"

"No, Luca. I mean Earth."

It was lucky that Luca had been sitting down, otherwise her legs may have failed to keep her upright. "But..."

"I know it's all a bit sudden, but the situation has dramatically changed. So much so that even Athena has communicated this to me in person. And you know it takes a lot for a QI to have a dialogue with an actual human."

Luca looked over at Dr. Rayman. "Is it true that the

QIs are becoming so detached from reality that they don't care about us anymore?"

"It may seem that way, but I don't know if it's true. Athena may be distant, but it does care. I think they have been preoccupied with these attacks by Node Runners, something that would seem impossible up until recently. Times are changing, Luca. We are entering a dark age, I fear."

"What about my parents? What are they saying about this?"

Dr. Rayman paused for a beat; her look became more serious and she leaned in across the counter. "The plan is for you to leave Earth and travel to the new O'Neill cylinder habitat they're building out in the asteroid belt, New World One. Out there you will be safe. Arrangements have been made, we leave tomorrow. That is, if you choose to go. No one's forcing you, Luca. But I would strongly advise it."

Luca gave the doctor a slow, considered look. Then she lowered her head and spoke in a low tone. "I've never told you this before, Steph, but I've wanted out of here for a long time. I never felt that I really belonged here. Childish as it may seem, I've always had this feeling that I was meant for better things."

"Don't worry, it passes with age." Dr. Rayman gave her a wry smile. "You'll need to get ready tonight and pack light, we leave in the morning. I'll pick you up and travel with you as far as the Johnston Transit Orbital. From there you're scheduled on a flight to New World One."

Luca glanced around her small apartment, cluttered with the accumulated detritus of her almost twenty-three years of life, and felt no great attachment to any of it. There were some friends and an on-off relationship she would miss, but nothing that really mattered. She looked out the window at the evening sky beyond. *But out there,* she thought, *is a chance to meet my family again and also see some of the wonders of the solar system.*

"What about all this?" She gestured around the room.

"Don't worry, it will all be packed up and sent on."

"And this?" Luca nudged the package resting on the counter between them.

"As I said, it's from Athena, so who knows what it could be. Although, it must be pretty special as very few people are ever given anything by a QI. So, all I can say is that you must matter a great deal to it." Dr. Rayman rose from the stool. "So it's agreed, I'll see you here around seven?"

Luca also stood up and came over to the doctor. She nodded. "Yes, let's do it."

They hugged for a moment, then Dr. Rayman headed out the door, leaving Luca to contemplate the contents of the enigmatic birthday present from the quantum intelligence, Athena.

4

FLY

It was some time after Dr. Rayman had left before Luca finally decided to open the package from Athena. Her initial reluctance was partly because since this was a birthday present, she should really wait until tomorrow when it was officially her birthday. But in reality, she was a little scared of what it might contain. After all, it was from a quantum intelligence so the contents of the package were likely to be very eccentric or even downright bizarre.

Yet when she examined the box, turning it over in her hands, Luca sensed that it contained an electronic device of some kind, as she could feel the infinitesimal current it radiated. This hypersensitivity to electromagnetic radiation that Luca possessed was both a gift and a curse. At work they called her the human voltmeter. Any time she had reason to enter a high-energy environment, every nerve in her body would tingle, and not in a pleasant way.

It was not that this hypersensitivity was dangerous, it was just extremely uncomfortable for her.

But she couldn't sleep. Instead she lay awake thinking about how all the great dislocations in her life had been because of the VanHeilding family, and here was yet another one. So, as dawn began to cast its pale light over the city skyline, Luca got up, made herself a coffee, and began examining the package.

On the top surface it had a fingerprint lock, so she placed her index finger on it and after a second it chimed, then the upper half of the case split in two and folded open. Nestled inside was an elegantly designed insect drone, about the size of her fully extended hand. It twitched, and Luca moved back a little, not quite knowing what to expect. The drone raised itself up on six spindly legs, arched its head toward Luca, and activated a laser scanner. A thin beam of light scrolled up across Luca's body, pausing momentarily over her eyes. It was doing a retinal scan, presumably to verify that the person opening the package was the rightful recipient.

Satisfied that the person before it was Luca, the outer casing on the back of the insect drone cracked open, extended a set of semi-translucent wings, and rose into the air. It hovered for a moment before settling back down on the counter just to one side of the packaging.

"Hello, my name is Fly and I have a message for you from Athena." Its voice was thin and slightly retro, but not unpleasant.

"Happy birthday, Luca. I am sorry that you have to

leave Earth, but I fear I am unable to provide you with the protection you need. No doubt you have heard about the increase in attacks on our network, not just in frequency but also in their audacity. This means that your safety has become uncertain and I have advised those who have your best interest at heart to make arrangements for your departure.

"As a parting gift, I have created this little drone to assist you on your travels. It can be operated via the neural lace enclosed.

"Please know that you have never been far from my thoughts ever since you arrived under my protection all those years ago. And so it is with great sadness that I bid you farewell."

The drone then deactivated itself, having finished the message. It sat mute on the breakfast counter, its wings folded, its strange eyes cold and lifeless.

Luca took a sip of coffee, then delicately extracted the neural lace—the mind-machine interface that controlled the drone—from its slot inside the package.

Why has Athena given me this? she wondered as she examined the neural interface. Athena was an all-knowing quantum intelligence, so surely it should be acutely aware of Luca's hypersensitivity to electrical current. She had always shunned the use of a neural lace; it was almost a phobia with her. Did Athena have some ulterior motive in giving her the one thing she most feared?

She examined the lace, turning it over in her hands. It

was not unlike a slim, curved comb that slid under the hairline at the base of the skull, wrapping around from ear to ear. Once in place and activated, thin electrode filaments would snake out from each of the prongs and make their way across the cranium, finding the sweet spots, and securing themselves through hair follicles. It was elegant and discreet, and it would be difficult to tell if someone was wearing one. Yet, as she examined it, she realized that this one could do much more than simply control a drone. It could theoretically interface with any system or data-stream, depending on the skill of the operator.

She placed it carefully back into its case and turned her attention to the drone itself, Fly. Luca, being a technologist, could appreciate the engineering and technical sophistication of the machine. She reached over and picked it up.

It was a little bigger than her hand and surprisingly light. Its thin wings had folded themselves up under the hard outer casing. Since it was an ornithopter, achieving flight by high-speed flapping, its wings were delicate and so needed protecting when not in use. She turned it over, examining its underside. Six spindly legs extended with multiple articulations. Two had clawed feet, the other four with pads like a gecko. These presumably gave it the ability to both cling to surfaces and manipulate objects. But the thing that most surprised Luca was a prominent bulge on its underbelly, indicating to her that it had a weapons system. She clicked on a desk light and leaned in to get a closer look.

A small nozzle protruded from the bulge. It was some class of projectile system. Laser or plasma would require too much energy for such a tiny device. *Darts?* she wondered. But for something this small, such a projectile would be useless, at best simply an irritation for the target. If this was the best protection Athena was offering her, then she was in deep trouble already.

She switched off the lamp, stowed the little drone back into its case along with the neural lace, and shoved it into her backpack. She checked the time: 6:50 am.

Soon, the ground car would arrive and she would be leaving this place, leaving the Institute, leaving her friends, leaving her whole life behind. Sneaking out at the break of dawn like a callous lover. She wondered if she should tell someone, let them know what she was doing. But Dr. Rayman had strictly forbade it, emphasizing the need for total secrecy. No communication whatsoever in case the Node Runners picked it up on the Grid and drilled down to her location.

As she sat there waiting, Luca once again began to lament the misfortune of her lineage. Why did she have to be a VanHeilding? Why could she not have been born into some mundane family, whose only mission in life was to just simply live it, not seek global domination? But this was her lot, her burden to bear, and she had been running and hiding most of her life. Now at least, she might get to see her parents again—that was something normal people did.

Her wrist tab pinged, indicating the approach of the ground car coming to collect her. She stood up, slung on her backpack, took one last look around her tiny apartment, and headed out the door.

OUTSIDE ON THE STREET, Luca wasn't sure if the battered wreck that vaguely resembled a ground car was really here for her. But it was the only one within sight, so it must be. Yet it was with some trepidation that she approached it. The side door swung open and to her surprise she realized it wasn't autonomous, as nearly all cars were.

"Hi Luca, sorry for the beat-up junker, but we couldn't risk an autonomous vehicle. That would mean a connection to the Grid." Dr. Rayman was sitting behind a set of complicated-looking manual controls.

"What museum did you extract this thing from?" Luca said as she clambered into the passenger seat.

"There are more of these machines on the roads than people realize. They're a rich person's hobby. You would be shocked to know how much this is worth."

"I'm sure I would." Luca cast a glance at the shabby interior.

"Better buckle up." Dr. Rayman started the ground car up again. "We have a rough ride ahead of us."

5

SHUTTLE PORT

An early morning sun broke over the mountains to the east, casting jagged shadows across the valley floor below. Dr. Stephanie Rayman slid down from her perch on top of a boulder, bringing with her a cloud of dust and sand.

"No sign of the shuttle, yet," she said as she patted the dust off her clothes and handed the binoculars to Luca. "Here, you take a look. Maybe you can see something I've missed."

It had taken them the best part of two hours to exit the city and make their way up through the mountains to the location of the old shuttle port. The ancient ground car struggled and wheezed its way along the back roads and dirt tracks, and she had felt that at any moment it would finally give up and die, leaving them stranded. But it got there in the end, helped along by copious four-letter encouragement from Dr. Rayman.

She had parked it a short distance from the derelict facility, high up on a side road from where they could scout out the area. A move Luca found disconcerting, considering that this shuttle had been arranged by Steph in the first place, so why all the caution? But Luca didn't quiz her about it, preferring instead to let the doctor do it her way. But now it seemed that the shuttle was nowhere to be seen. Not a good start.

Luca took the binoculars and scrambled up the side of the boulder. She lay flat on her belly and scanned the desert valley below, zeroing in on the old, abandoned shuttle port—most of which had been reclaimed by the ever-encroaching desert. Great dunes covered most of its landing pads and many of the buildings. Here and there she could make out the corners and edges of structures sticking out of the sand, where they had not been fully digested by the dunes.

Yet the central pad had survived mostly intact, enough for a medium-sized shuttle to land. But it was deserted, nothing but dust and scrawny weeds.

Luca put the glasses down and turned her head to call down to Steph. "So when's it supposed to be here?"

"A half-hour ago. I was expecting it to just be sitting there, waiting for us when we arrived."

"You think something happened to them?"

"Probably not. But you have to remember that a crew willing to smuggle a person off-planet, no questions asked, are by their very nature not the most reliable. And if they've backed out of the deal then that must mean word is out."

"Word of what?"

"Luca, are you a complete idiot? You, of course. Do you think this is all a game? Why are we were using a rust bucket to get here, and carrying no tech that's hooked into the Grid?" She gave Luca a stern look.

Luca was silent for a moment, considering Steph's outburst. "What do we do now?"

"We wait and see if they arrive. Maybe they've just been delayed."

Luca nodded, then she had an idea. "Why don't you use Fly to scout out the place?" she said as she scrambled down the boulder to Steph.

"I can't—but you could. The neural interface is coded to your DNA. Only you can use it."

"Eh...I don't know if I can. You know what I'm like with that sort of direct brain communication, it gives me the heebie-jeebies."

"Hey, it's just a drone. It's not like you're becoming a Node Runner."

Luca hesitated. The last time she tried using a direct mind-machine interface, it had not gone well. But that was her experimenting with a direct connection to the Grid, resulting in too much data flooding into her mind and major neural overload. During the brief period she was connected, she thought she would lose her mind completely. She had pulled herself out again almost immediately, and vowed never to try it again. But Steph was right, this was just a drone, and a very sophisticated one at that. Luca had to admit that she was tempted.

She screwed her mouth up and looked over at the ground car where her backpack was stored. "Okay," she finally said. "I'll give it a go. But if I start to panic, please promise me you'll pull me out, take off the lace."

"Sure, of course." Steph gave her a solemn nod. "But you'll be fine. And it would be good to know what's down there before we go walking in."

Luca retrieved her pack from the car and carefully extracted the drone. She placed it on top of the hood and then fished out the neural lace, the interface that operated the machine. She hesitated for a beat as she considered what might await her on the other side, so to speak. She also felt Steph's eyes on her, watching and waiting to see if she would actually do it.

Luca looked over at her. "Okay, here goes." She opened the case, took out the neural lace, and slid it up under the hairline at the base of her skull. Immediately it recognized her DNA signature and began to activate; thin filaments extruded from the device and began to seek out connection points around her cranium. To Luca it felt like an infestation of head lice, and she resisted the urge to whip it off again.

But then her mind felt a new clarity emerging, it had a sharpness to it, yet it came with an increasing sense of anxiety. Luca fought to keep control of her urge to disconnect—it was just a drone she was interfacing with, nothing more. But if this was how she felt connecting to a simple machine, what must be going on in the head of a Node Runner? The thought made her shudder.

She took a few deep breaths and calmed herself down. In her mind's eye, she began to see the broad sweep of the desert and realized Fly had activated itself and risen high up overhead. She concentrated, focusing on the threads of connectivity connecting her to the drone. She could feel them, like the strings of a marionette, thin filaments of control that she tugged and manipulated.

"See anything?" Steph's voice entered her consciousness, and Luca took a moment to reassign her mind to the here and now.

"Yes, it's...amazing."

"What is?"

But Luca didn't answer, so wrapped up had she become in the sweeping grace of the drone, like a bird on the wind, a great condor seeking out its prey. Then, for no apparent reason that Luca could discern, a great river of anxiety rushed over her mind and she panicked. The desert sand came racing toward her; she was losing control, not concentrating, her panic rose as she sought to regain control.

"Luca, what the hell are you play at? It's going to crash."

But before she could regain control, the drone

snapped out of the dive and rose again, and Luca sensed that she was no longer fully interfaced with it. The machine must have instigated some failsafe protocol, protecting itself from destruction.

"My apologies, Luca. But I can't allow you to destroy me. Athena would not be very happy if that happened on my first outing."

Luca froze for a beat as she tried to make sense of the voice in her head—and it was in her head, wasn't it? She looked around to see Steph standing beside her, hand shading her eyes as she tracked the drone's path across the sky.

"Yes, it is me, Fly, the drone."

Can it read my mind? she thought. But by now, the drone had returned and settled itself back on the hood of the ground car. Luca looked at it for a moment before deactivating the neural lace. Instantly, a dullness descended, like some great cloud mass had obscured the sun.

"Did you see anything?" Steph's voice came at her like a blunt instrument.

Luca rubbed the back of her neck and tried to reorient herself. "Yes, no... I..."

She felt Steph's hand on her shoulder. "You okay?"

Luca lifted her head. "Yeah, I'm fine. That was a bit of a head-rush. I'd forgotten just how overwhelming a neural interface can be. But I'm okay. And no, I didn't manage to spot anything, but I'm not doing that again... not for a while."

The two stood there for a moment looking down at the ruins of the abandoned shuttle port. Then Steph shifted and jerked a finger at the horizon. "Luca, over there. I see it, it's coming in to land. Looks like they were just delayed, that's all."

6

CAPT. WEISMANN

L uca and Steph watched the shuttle slow its descent, twisting around gently as it came in to land on the central pad. Great billowing clouds of dust kicked up by its retro-thrusters engulfed the craft. It disappeared almost entirely from view for a brief moment, before the wind blowing in across the plateau began to disperse the cloud.

Luca packed up Fly and was about to remove the neural lace when Steph stopped her. "Hold up a moment, Luca. Let's check this out a bit more."

"I'm not operating Fly again, if that's what you think."

Steph didn't reply. She had the binoculars up to her eyes, focusing on the activity down at the shuttle.

The dust had settled by now, and the side airlock had opened, disgorging two of the crew. One scanned the surroundings while the other seemed to be checking something on the hull of the craft.

"Okay," said Steph as she put away the binoculars. "That's them alright. Come on, let's get down there before they change their minds."

Luca grabbed her backpack and they clambered back into the old ground car. Steph started it up with a rattle and headed off down the track. As they approached the shuttle pad, Steph rolled down the side window and shouted out to one of the crew. "You finally got here. For a while there you had me worried."

He walked over to the car with a casual swagger, stretching his arms and shoulders as he moved. "Of course we're here. I never miss a chance to stretch my legs in one-gee." He then gave an expansive gesture with his hands. "And to breathe in all this splendid air." He made a show of inhaling deeply. "Ahhh...wonderful."

"Any problems?" Steph glanced over to where some of the crew were inspecting damage on the craft's hull.

"We had a few...issues to deal with on the way, that's why we got held up. But all is good now."

This seemed to satisfy Steph. "I'm going to hide this rust bucket over in one of those hangars." She pointed off in the direction of a dilapidated structure, one corner of which had collapsed, but the entrance was still big enough for the car to fit through. "Then we can get the show on the road."

"Sure thing, Dr. Rayman." He then shifted his gaze to Luca, studying her for a moment before giving her a lazy salute.

When they moved off, Luca turned to Steph. "I don't trust that guy."

"Like I said, Luca, getting you off-planet without being noticed means dealing with the likes of Capt. Andre Weismann and his crew. But he's okay, just a little rough around the edges."

"Like his ship—a lot of dents and scorch marks on the hull. Are you sure that thing can fly?"

"Don't worry, it's a solid craft. It will get us to the Transit Orbital no problem." She brought the car to a stop, as far inside a deserted hangar as she could go.

"All right, let get going. Car should be fine here. Can't see anyone finding it for an age. Just make sure you bring everything. Don't leave anything that could link us to it, just in case it's found eventually. And here, take this." Steph fished a small PEP weapon, a pulsed energy projectile device, from her jacket and handed it to Luca.

She took it warily, examining it with a sense of trepidation. "Why do I need this?"

"Hey, Luca, it's a big bad solar system out there." Steph pointed off to the distant sky. "Don't believe the warm fuzzy, shiny rainbow shit they tell you about all the fabulous glories of our spacefaring race. Humans are still humans, and there's plenty of scum out there. So just take it, hide it. Hopefully you won't have to use it. You do know how to use one of these, don't you?"

Luca turned the PEP pistol over in her hands. "Yeah, you forget my mother is Miranda. She deemed it a primary part of my education."

"Okay, keep it on stun and you won't accidentally kill anyone with it, unless of course you want to."

Luca slipped the weapon into her jacket. "All this isn't filling me with confidence, Steph."

"It's just a precaution. Once we get you to the Transit Orbital and packed off on a ship to the New World, you'll be safe then."

THE SIDE CARGO ramp was down when they returned to the shuttle and Luca spotted Capt. Weismann just inside the entrance. He seemed to be exchanging heated words with another of the crew. She couldn't catch any of what they were arguing over, but she thought she heard *money* being mentioned. The argument stopped abruptly when the other guy caught sight of Luca and Steph approaching the cargo ramp. He disappeared into the interior of the craft, leaving Weismann to greet them at the entrance.

"Trouble?" said Steph, flicking her head in the direction of the ship's interior.

"Naw...just the usual bullshit complaining." He waved a dismissive hand. "Goes with the job. Come on, let's get you stashed and we'll be on our way."

They moved in through the airlock and the ramp rose up behind them.

IT WAS A STANDARD CARGO TRANSPORT, albeit one that had

seen better days, and typical of a thousand others just like it, all designed to bring people and goods in and out of Earth's gravity well. Big enough to be useful, but small enough that they could land pretty much anywhere there was a reasonably-sized flat patch. Half a football field would do, in a pinch.

They were powered by a fusion reactor feeding energy into four plasma engines, mounted one on each corner. These cantilevered to produce downward thrust for takeoff and landing. But once airborne, the engines would swing up to produce forward thrust. Small stubby wings also helped provide lift and flight control in Earth's atmosphere up as far as the Karman line.

At least a third of its internal volume was taken up with the fusion reactor and ancillary systems, the rest was cargo bay, with a small four-person flight deck. The cargo bay in this class of ship could be fitted out in a hundred different ways, but this one had a number of small crew cabins along with a few additional seats for passengers. Luca got the sense that this crew lived on the ship—it was their home.

"This way, better get your gear stored and get strapped in." Weismann pointed to some passenger seats just aft of the flight deck. "We're going to be taking some heavy gee on takeoff, so grab a barf bag if you're the type to throw up. Nothing worse than a load of puke misting up the cabin in zero-gee."

"How long is the flight?" Luca asked.

"We'll be out of Earth's gravity and into zero-gee in a

few minutes. Then another two hours to get to the Johnston Transit Orbital—give or take." He gave a hand gesture for emphasis. "We'll need to...eh, come in through the back door, so to speak. Dock at one of the old, decommissioned sections."

Weismann left them to get strapped in as he ascended the companionway to the flight deck. Steph turned to Luca and gave her a comforting nod. "We'll soon be there. After that it should get a little easier. We won't have to deal with these...privateers."

7

THE HOLD

They were nearly an hour into the journey, having broken free of Earth's gravity some forty minutes ago. Luca, being bored, had unstrapped her seat harness and floated freely in the cargo hold of the shuttle. Dr. Rayman chose to remain strapped in while Luca entertained herself by bouncing around from handhold to handhold.

"You should try this, Steph, it's a lot of fun."

"You forget, I've spent a great many years bouncing around in space. All I want to do now is feel solid ground beneath my feet."

Luca was in mid-flight between one side of the cargo hold and the other, a particularly adventurous move for her. She was gaining in confidence and reckoned she could pull this one off and land dead on target on the other side. But a sudden change in the thrust vector of the shuttle sent her careening into the cockpit bulkhead.

"What the... They've changed direction?" She managed to grab hold of a handle just as the flight deck door burst open and Capt. Weismann came flying out, followed by the copilot holding a plasma weapon. It took Luca a moment to realize that the captain was not moving—either he was dead or unconscious. The copilot was now followed out by the two other crew, one of whom began gathering up the inert captain. The copilot swung his weapon on Luca.

"Change of plan, ladies. You're now going to be making a very large contribution to our retirement fund." He looked over at the other two crew, who were nodding and smiling their approval.

"Too right. Enough of this chump-change, people-smuggling crap." This came from a crew member who was now strapping the captain's limp body into a vacant seat.

"Turns out that there is a pretty penny being offered for you, seeing as you're a VanHeilding. And it looks like they want their little girl back."

"That's not the deal." Steph had unfastened herself from the seat. "The deal was to take us to the Johnston Transit Orbital."

"That might have been the deal with Andre over there. But guess what, he's not in charge anymore, is he? So now we have a new deal, one where we get some real money."

"Screw you." Steph whipped a plasma pistol out from

inside her jacket with impressive speed and turned it on the copilot. But she wasn't quick enough. He fired a blast, hitting her square on the chest and sending her flying backward.

"Steph, no," Luca screamed out as she made a lunge for the copilot. But she wasn't quick enough either, and received a vicious blow to the forehead from the butt of pistol. She too went spinning backward, her head a rage of pain, slowly losing consciousness.

"Don't kill her," someone shouted. "We need her alive."

∾

LUCA AWOKE to a pounding headache and momentary spasm of terror. A deep primal desire to cry out welled up inside her, but she fought the urge, and instead she took a moment to try and orient herself and regain some sense of location. She was enveloped in complete darkness, or maybe she was blind. But to her relief, she began to make out the faint illumination of various systems indicators, multicolored pinpricks of light in otherwise complete darkness. So she wasn't blind. But how far or how near these dots of light were was impossible for her to discern.

She was strapped into a seat, still in zero-gee, this much she could tell. But was it the same shuttle, or some other ship? *It might be the same ship,* she thought.

Luca tried to move, but her hands and feet were tied.

Still, she could reach the harness release, but when she punched it nothing happened; it had been locked, no way out.

"Steph," she whispered, hoping to get a reply. Even a groan would do. Silence. "Steph," she tried again, this time a little louder. Still nothing.

The effort made her head hurt, and she lifted her bound hands to feel the side of her forehead where the copilot had struck her. It was raw and tender with a mass of blood caked down past her cheek. She moved her hand around her head to try and ease the pain, and felt a finger touch something. It was the neural interface. She was still wearing it. The shuttle crew hadn't noticed. So, with a deep sense of trepidation, she extended a finger and activated it.

Instantly, Luca felt the filaments extending out across her skull seeking out contact points, clarity blossoming in her mind as they made their connections. Yet all she could sense was darkness.

Was the drone active? Was it destroyed? She couldn't tell, so she simply whispered its name. "Fly?"

"Yes." The reply was instantaneous, shocking her by its presence in her head. A spark of excited fear rippled through her body, and she fought to contain it. "Where are you?"

"I am in your backpack."

"Can you get out? But be careful, don't let anyone see you."

"I am already out."

"I don't see anything. Why can't I see what you see?"

"Because there is no illumination. Wait, switching to night vision."

With that, an eerie green luminescence began to bloom in her mind's eye, and physical details began to emerge. Luca now focused on getting Fly to look around the area, stopping when she saw a bright body shape strapped into a seat. Was the drone looking at her? She moved her head from side to side; the body did the same.

"That's me. You're in the same room. Can you fly over here and cut me loose?"

"I cannot fly in zero-gee—but I can crawl over to you."

Luca focused her mind on maneuvering the drone, and soon had it moving along the wall by hopping and grabbing on to anything that it could use. Finally, when it was close enough, it jumped over to her seat and began cutting through her bonds with its claws. She rubbed her wrists to get some feeling back in to her hands as Fly went to work on the bonds around her ankles, and then moved on to the seat harness.

All this neural activity made her stomach churn. It was a response to the inability of her brain to square the circle between her physical self and what the drone was seeing. She closed her eyes, but that didn't help much since she was receiving the visual feed directly through the neural lace.

The skin on her scalp tingled with a hundred tiny

pinpricks as the lace deepened its connections. The more she interacted with the drone, striving to bend it to her will, the more connections the lace made, subdividing and multiplying its points of contact. Her stomach began to settle but her sense of dislocation intensified, and with it came that same old visceral fear of losing her mind to the interface.

She took a few deep breaths and fought it down. She had no choice. If she were to have any chance of getting out of here, then the drone was her only option. She had to dig deep, feel the fear, let it ride over her, she had to give herself over to the mind-machine interface. Luca practiced the routines she had learned to invoke whenever this fear rose within her. She had been in this situation before, a long time ago when she was only seven years old, an experience that had indelibly etched itself into her subconscious with deep lines of trauma, an endless source of bad dreams ever since.

They had snatched her while on a school trip to Rongo City on Ceres. Picked her off from the edge of the group as the thirty or so kids made their way through a busy central market, like a pack of wolves picking off a straggler from the herd. They bundled her into a waiting ground car and drugged her. She awoke some time later to pretty much the same scenario as she found herself in now. Strapped into a seat in a spacecraft with her feet and hands bound, weightless in space.

But they didn't get far. The ship was tracked and then

intercepted by a frigate out of Ceres run and operated by a well-armed cohort of mercenaries in the pay of the government of the Belt Federation. They implemented a search and rescue mission not from any desire to do the right thing, but for the bounty that had been put up by her family for her safe return. It helped that those instigating the crime had made enough mistakes that their trail could be followed. The ship was tracked to a location in orbit around the dwarf planet while it was waiting for another ship to rendezvous. But the mercenaries had found them first. And so, less than four hours after her kidnap, they had hacked their way in and killed everyone on board and rescued her.

Yet for Luca, the entire episode was traumatic in the extreme, and for a long time after she would refuse to leave the safety of her own room, angrily protesting against any attempt to coax her out. She did eventually manage to reenter the outside world through a combination of her father's emotional support, her mother's efforts to beef up security infrastructure, and simple youthful resilience.

But it soon became clear to Scott and Miranda that this was really no life for a child, so they decided to pack her off to where she would be free from the threat posed by the VanHeilding family and have some chance of living a normal life. The downside was that they could not go with her. And so at the tender age of eight, she was shipped off to Earth into the hands of family friends, under the protection of the quantum intelligence Athena. For Luca, that one event all those years ago was responsible for ruining her childhood and breaking up her family.

And here she was, fifteen years later, and VanHeilding was still trying to screw her life up.

8

CURARE

By now, a new resolve had built up in Luca's mind. She was not going to be a victim. She had been running and hiding, and she was sick of it. If breaking herself free of this situation meant having to face down her fear of the neural interface, well so be it. These bastards were not going to mess her life up anymore. She concentrated, and as she did her scalp began to tingle.

First, she needed to know what this drone was capable of. It was semiautonomous and she could verbally communicate with it, that much she knew. She started by simply asking it a few questions in her mind.

"Can you communicate with Athena?"

"Negative," came the response. "That would constitute a security flaw and could be used as a way to track you down, assuming there are Node Runners sniffing the Grid for your signature."

"Well, too late now," she thought.

"Indeed," it replied. "The only comms interface is the neural lace you are currently utilizing."

"Weapons?"

"I'm glad you asked. I have a pneumatic projectile system, loaded with thirty curare-tipped barbs."

"Curare, is that not a bit...primitive?"

"It worked pretty well for the native tribes of the Amazon rainforest when they wanted to paralyze their prey. Rather an inspired weapon for a lightweight flying drone such as myself, don't you think?"

"I guess so. Does it kill?"

"No. The victim will suffer complete paralysis for several hours depending on body mass. After which they should make a full recovery. Although I should warn you, it takes a minute or two to take effect, so it's more of a stealth weapon."

Luca's interrogation continued like this for a while until she had a reasonable understanding of the little drone's capabilities. Now it was time to put it to good use.

It couldn't fly in zero-gee, but it did have six legs, two with small claws for manipulating objects. The rest were tipped with a kind of pad designed like the feet of a gecko. This enabled it to stick to pretty much any surface. It crawled off Luca's lap, across the floor, and up the side wall of the cabin. It paused for a beat as it quickly disassembled the cover of a ventilation duct. The cover floated free, and the drone scuttled inside.

Luca was seeing what it saw. Fly moved only a short

distance, not more than the length of its body, and peered through another slatted ventilation cover into an identical cabin to the one Luca was trapped in. It was also dark, no illumination. But the night vision of the drone picked out a ghostly figure also tied up in a seat. It was Dr. Rayman, and she was still alive; Luca could see her struggling with her bonds. But Luca instructed the drone to ignore the doctor for the moment and keep moving.

After a short distance, she could see pale light filtering into the duct from another vent, and instructed the drone to crawl toward it, adjusting the night vision to accommodate for the increased illumination. Fly peered through the slats into the main cargo hold. None of the crew could be seen, so it proceeded to disassemble the cover, carefully retracting it back inside so it would not float off across the cargo hold and alert some crew member. A moment or two later, it was out of the shaft and making its way to the flight deck.

Luca had been so taken up with operating the drone that she had no resurgence of the anxiety the neural interface normally induced in her. Of course, this sudden realization now caused a momentary pang of fear, and her fluid interaction with the drone faltered. Yet it was the drone that brought her back; its needs became prominent in her mind, like the way a new dog owner might find themselves focused on the needs of the pet and less on their own self-indulgence.

"What is my objective?" The thoughts of the drone entered Luca's mind.

"Eh...locate the crew without being spotted." This was not spoken, it was simply the primary thought in Luca's mind, now transferred as a directive to the drone. This was also a moment of revelation for her, as she realized that the drone did not need to be micromanaged. Luca did not need to control its mechanical function, she simply needed to interface with its mind. A sense of excitement bubbled up inside her as she began to focus on the data-stream coming into her from the drone. She felt as if she had an extension to her body, a sixth sense.

The drone crawled across the forward bulkhead on the ship, inching its way to the open doorway for the flight deck. It paused at the edge and angled itself to scan the area. One crew member sat asleep in the pilot seat, his head slightly to one side, his arms floating freely. Another crew member occupied the nav-station, and looked to be studying a 3D schematic of this particular sector of space. The third and final crew member was checking weapons.

Luca now interrogated the drone's mind to analyze the probability of it taking out all three crew while evading detection, given that the drug-tipped barbs would take time to have the desired effect. It analyzed angles of attack, target position, and body mass of each crew member. It also calculated its lines of escape should it be detected. Fly finally arrived at a 76% probability of success.

However, this still left Luca with a problem. Assuming the drone could disable the crew, then what?

She had no clue how to pilot a spaceship. It would be still heading to wherever the crew had plotted and she would be helpless to alter that. But Dr. Rayman, on the other hand, had years of experience on spaceships, although that was in the capacity of the ship's medical doctor, so her piloting skills could be limited, if any.

Luca now regretted not freeing Steph when she had the chance. At least then she could have asked her. She considered sending the drone back, but could miss this chance to take out the crew while they were resting and distracted. It might be the worst mistake of her life. *No, best just take control,* she thought. It was an instruction for the drone to advance.

Fly considered its targets and chose the one checking weapons to go down first. It moved stealthily into the flight deck, narrowing the distance to the target to maximize its projectile accuracy. Two barbs shot out of its underbelly in quick succession...*phitt, phitt.* The action by the drone went unheard against the background hum of the ship's systems.

"What the...?" The crew member slapped his neck as if swatting a mosquito. He then delicately fingered the sting and gently pulled out a two-centimeter-long stainless steel needle and held it up to examine it.

The guy on the nav-station glanced over to see what had startled his comrade. *Phitt...phitt.* Two more projectiles embedded themselves in the navigator's forehead. He flinched with the impact, more from surprise than pain. "Damnit, I think I've been stung. We must have picked up a load of bugs when we landed in that desert? I hate bugs."

"It's not a bug, you moron, I think we're being hunted by...something." He started looking around for the source of the projectiles. "You'd better wake up the Cap." He gestured toward the still sleeping figure, then picked up his weapon.

"What do you mean, not a bug?"

"I think...it's—" He put a hand up to his throat; his mouth moved, but no words came out. Then his eyes rolled back in his head and he went limp, floating freely inside the flight deck.

Fly now moved out from its hiding place and scuttled along the side wall to get a better angle on the captain.

"Holy crap." The navigator recoiled in horror at the sight of this mechanical insect. But Fly paid him no notice, and fired two darts into the neck of the still sleeping captain.

At the same moment, Luca unstrapped the seat harness and floated out of the cabin and into the adjoining one. It was dark, but there was just enough ambient light filtering through the open door to make out the bound figure of the doctor. "Steph?"

There was a brief pause as Dr. Rayman oriented herself to the source of the voice. "Luca? What the...?"

"Yes, it's me. I've come to get you out of here." Luca went to work on the straps.

"The crew?" Steph whispered.

"Don't worry... Fly took care of them. It turns out that

it comes with a weapons system, poison darts." She tapped her skull. "And they didn't realize I still had a neural lace, so I booted it up and went to work."

"Are they dead?" By now Steph was free and floating out of the seat.

"No, no...curare. They're asleep for a few hours."

The two of them floated out of the cabin and made their way up to the flight deck, where they were greeted with the sight of the three crew floating freely and peacefully.

"I suppose we'd better get these guys stored away," Luca said as she started maneuvering one of the floating bodies.

"Those double-crossing bastards." Dr. Rayman was pissed. "I'm tempted to just blow them out the airlock."

THEY TOOK some time to remove all their weapons and then locked them inside a large, empty cargo container. Eventually, Luca and Steph floated back to the flight deck and Luca strapped herself into the pilot seat. She glanced at the bewildering array of controls and monitors. "This may seem like a stupid question, Steph. But I don't suppose you know how to fly a spaceship?"

9

GRAVITY POVERTY

The juggernaut-class ore carrier began its final burn, slowing itself down as it prepared to enter a parking position close to New World One, the gigantic O'Neill cylinder being constructed in Belt space. It was carrying over three-hundred thousand cubic meters of powered steel: mined, smelted, and processed out past the Vesta sector of the asteroid belt where the majority of the resources needed for the mammoth construction project originated.

Shortly, the ship would take its position in a queue and wait for the small transports to unload its cargo and take it to a bunkering station. From there it would be fed into the massive 3D printers that had been working nonstop for the last five Earth years, building the outer skin of the cylinder.

Scott McNabb punched the sector coordinates he had been given into his flight console, sat back, and let the onboard AI navigate the ship to their designated position in the queue. He glanced up at the main cockpit monitor and could see at least two other ore carriers ahead of him. Yet what dominated his view through the cockpit window was the gargantuan glistening O'Neill cylinder floating gracefully in the vastness of space.

NEW WORLD ONE, or simply the New World, as it was sometimes called, was the largest object ever created by humanity, and then some. A massive cylinder, eight kilometers in diameter and thirty long—at least it would be when it was finished. Currently, it was a mere fifteen kilometers long with only the first five habitable. The next five were currently being brought online, doubling the habitable space inside. The entire structure spun at a gentle twenty-eight revolutions per hour, facilitating a very comfortable one-gee environment along the inner rim. For those who lived and worked throughout the asteroid belt region, it was the promise of a little bit of heaven. A home away from home. Some even argued that it was better than the real thing.

In terms of mineral resources, the Belt wanted for nothing; it was the treasure trove of the solar system, a source of great wealth. In the early days of its exploration and exploitation, it was the risk-takers, the buccaneers that ventured out here and took on the challenges. Private space exploration companies like AsterX, Xaing Zu, and a great many others grew rich on the bounty of the asteroid belt. And as time went by, more and more people came to live and work in this narrow band of the solar system, and like all frontiersmen and women throughout history, conditions were brutal. But the worst was lack of gravity.

The Belt had mineral resources in abundance, but what it didn't have was a planet worthy of the name. Yes, there was Ceres, which might have been classified as a dwarf planet, but it had one-fifth the mass of Earth's moon, Luna. Its primary population center, Rongo, had less than twenty-five thousand inhabitants, most of whom were crammed into a series of complex centrifugal ringed habitats. This provided them with a reasonable two-thirds gravity, but conditions were cramped and utilitarian at best.

For those working for the many mining corporations, they lived between the zero-gee of the worksite and sabbaticals back on corporate orbitals, providing their workers with the minimum half-gee—a requirement stipulated by the Government of the Belt Federation Territories. Like the main population center on the dwarf planet, these orbital space stations were cramped and functional. And like all mining towns since the beginning of time, no one chose to live in them long term. They all arrived seeking their fortune, or at least the opportunity to make good money for a while. No one started out with the intention of staying, although, through the vagaries of fortune, many lost souls were destined never to leave.

Yet, if the Belt were to become anything more than

just a gargantuan mining town, then something needed to be done to address their primary shortcoming, that being lack of gravity. To this end, both government and private sector knocked their heads together, and through an arduous series of exploratory sessions it was proposed that they collaborate and construct New World One. A city in space. One that would comfortably accommodate several million inhabitants. It would put the Belt on the map, so to speak, and shift the balance of power away from Earth and Mars. Not only that, but it would draw in people from far and wide, not simply those working in mining or one of the related industries, but a whole new breed of citizens that chose to make a new life for themselves and their families in a grand futuristic utopia, or so the story went.

Yet some simply saw it as a great white elephant, a ridiculous project born more from the possession of vast wealth and hubris than from some grand vision for the future of humanity. And in the early stages of the project, this became the general consensus. No sooner was the first rivet cast, the in-fighting began between the various vested interests, all looking for more control. But after six months into construction, things began to settle down and as the project began to take shape, a new resolve emerged by all parties to settle their differences, lest it scupper what was beginning to look less like an expensive folly and more like a truly inspired creation.

So, after five years of construction, the first five kilometers of New World One were almost ready for full habitation, with a further five kilometers due for completion in the next few months. Soon there would be a mass exodus off Ceres, Vesta, and several other smaller colonies into the new habitat. The entire government of the Belt would migrate, along with all its administrative infrastructure including the quantum intelligence, Homer, which controlled this sector of Belt space. It would be a tricky time; they would be exposed and vulnerable to any shenanigans by Earth-based interests, who for one reason or another did not want to see the balance of power shift away from them.

Already, the news of the attack on the Grid Node had gotten people jittery. It was not the loss of the physical infrastructure that mattered so much as the fact that it had been done. For decades, people had lived under the supposed invulnerable protection that the QIs offered. But no longer. The attack showed that they could be bested. It was a shock to all; now, no one felt secure. If a key piece of infrastructure like that could be taken out, then nothing was safe.

To add to the pervading paranoia that was now spreading throughout the system, a heavily armed ship from the VanHeilding Corporation was rumored to be leaving Earth's orbit. To what purpose, no one knew.

10

AFTER THE FACT

Scott was hoping for a little R&R after this trip. Maybe take a shuttle over to the Sky Orbital Hotel and hang out for a few days, get scrubbed up, and enjoy the comforts of full-gee for a while. God knew he'd earned it. This was his seventh trip ferrying material for the New World project without a break, and this last trip was the worst. He had to do a collection from Andeluna, a godforsaken mining outpost at the ass-end of the asteroid belt, and to make matters worse some idiot sideswiped the local relay beacon for that sector, taking the whole thing offline. That meant everyone's comms were down, and navigation had to be done the old-fashioned way—no easy task when everything in the solar system kept changing position. Still, he was here now and looking forward to some rest, no more deep space travel for a week or two.

His rumination was broken by an alert from the

comms console informing him that the ship had reconnected with the local relay beacon and was downloading all cached data. The screen began to scroll with line after line of alerts, reports, and updates. He gave it a cursory glance, looking for anything that might require his response, yet not expecting much, when one line jumped out and grabbed his undivided attention. It was a message from Miranda, someone he had not heard from for over a year. It was followed by two other messages from her. He sat up in the seat, leaned over, and was about to tap the first of the highlighted messages when he hesitated.

What the hell does she want? he thought. He scanned the date on the first message—ten days ago. Then two more three days later. These would have arrived when he was around midway into his trip.

Hmmmm... Nothing for over a year, now three in a row. This can't be good. With a gathering sense of foreboding, Scott's finger hit the icon to bring the first message up on the comms monitor.

"Hi Scott, we need to talk about Luca."

Typical, he thought. *Straight to the point, no "how are you" or "how's it going" or "hope you're doing fine." No, just down to business.*

"A situation is rapidly developing back on Earth," the message continued. "There's been an attack on a major Grid Node in Athena's sector. Word is that it was orchestrated by VanHeilding using a cohort of neuralists —Node Runners, they call them. They were putting on a show, letting everyone know they can hack the Grid and disrupt the QI network."

Scott was used to Miranda and her conspiracy theories, but even he recognized the threat inherent in such an attack. But why hadn't he heard about it? Something like this would be big news. Then he realized it must have happened when his ship was in blackout.

"So," continued Miranda. "I've contacted Athena and…well, the QI is spooked. I never thought I would say this, but I think it's having a crisis of confidence, like it can't be sure of the data-stream anymore." She paused for a beat.

"The thing is, Scott, do we pull Luca out? I know we've been over this a hundred times before, but part of me thinks she's not safe there anymore. So, we need to talk, and soon. Get back to me as fast as you can, we need to make a decision. Bye."

"Goddamnit," Scott shouted out as he raised his hands to his forehead and ran his fingers through his hair. A tsunami of fear began to race through his mind. Left to her own devices, Miranda had the potential to overreact to any threat posed by her estranged family. Not that her fears were not without foundation; the VanHeildings were a dangerous and powerful lot, and they had attempted more than once to kidnap Luca—for what reason neither he nor Miranda could fathom. But the threat was real, not simply a figment of Miranda's imagination.

It was after the last attempt that Scott had been

persuaded to sequester Luca on Earth under the protection of the QI, Athena. Dr. Stephanie Rayman had remained on Earth after the fight to connect Athena to the QI network, and had established a science institute there. She was ready and willing to take on the task, and Luca would be out of harm's way—as she had been up until now, it seemed.

Yet, even though she was safe, losing her had driven a wedge between Scott and Miranda. Her reaction to that loss was an ever-increasing anger toward her family and what they stood for, but more than that, the kidnapping attempt had left her feeling vulnerable. And so she became ever more security conscious, to the point where she had built up her own squad of mercenaries that surrounded her. Well-trained ex-military people she had known back in the day. She was building a small army, and Scott wanted no part of it. So, one day, completely out of the blue, Cyrus had offered him a contract skippering a frigate for his blossoming construction empire. Scott didn't think twice; he took it and never looked back.

Miranda didn't seem to care, as least that's how Scott saw it. Still, as time went on, she mellowed. She turned her private army into a private security business, ferrying the rich and powerful around the solar system in her luxury ship, Perception.

Best of luck to her, was Scott's feeling on the matter. But it was not his idea of fun, not that ferrying ore was a barrel of laughs either, but at least he didn't get shot at.

He hit the icon for Miranda's next message.

"Look, Scott, you need to talk to me. I know we've had our...differences, but this is serious. My sources are telling me there's an all-out attack planned on a QI by VanHeilding and these Node Runners. If Athena goes down then Luca is exposed, and you know what that means. Please respond as soon as possible."

Scott checked the timestamp on the message; it was six days old. *She must think I just don't care,* he thought, and tapped the icon for the next message from Miranda. This one was only fourteen hours after the previous one.

"Why have you not gotten back to me? You don't seem to understand the urgency. I can't wait for you any longer. I sorry, but I'm taking unilateral action and working on a plan to get Luca out. We can't wait until after whatever VanHeilding is planning has happened. It needs to be done now. Steph has agreed to help. I can't say more since our communications may be compromised—who knows what these Node Runners are capable of?"

There was a momentary pause in the message, and Scott could hear an exasperated sigh. "Just...talk to me, Scott. Stop this...running away all the time." Another pause, another sigh. "Anyway, I'll keep you posted. I don't know why, but I suppose Luca would want me to."

Scott felt a deep wave of apprehension mixed with frustration ripple through him. None of this would have happened if that relay beacon had not been put out of commission. He could have persuaded Miranda to stay her hand, leave Luca where she was, not start taking drastic action, at least until the actual threat could be determined. But no, now she had gone and let her paranoia run away with her.

He looked down at the console and saw yet another message from Miranda. This was around four days later, presumably to give him an update on Luca's new location.

"Scott, eh...there's been a...complication. Neither Luca nor Steph arrived at the rendezvous point, the Johnston Transit Orbital. They took off from Earth as planned, but there has been no sighting of them yet. They should have arrived...seventeen hours ago."

She gave a long sigh. "Look, I know what you're going to say, but save it, because we may have a problem on our hands. I'm going to give it another ten hours or so, and if there is still no sign of them, then I'll instruct Max, the AI here on Perception, to chart a course for Earth's orbit, to the last known location. I swear I'm not going to let anything happen to her even if it's the last thing I do. I will find her, Scott, believe me when I say that. I will find her." She went silent for a while, and Scott assumed the message must be finished, but she had one last thing to say. "Okay, okay, maybe I screwed up, but at least I'm here doing something. At least I give a shit." The message finally ended.

By now, Scott was apoplectic. How could she do this after everything they had been through to keep Luca safe? It had defined their lives and cost them so much. But he knew Miranda would do something like this, such was her hatred. Ever since he'd met her, she'd been fighting a one-woman war against her family, particularly against its patriarch, her father Fredrick VanHeilding. And now it seemed she had lost.

He flicked open the coms and recorded a message for her.

"Miranda, just got your messages. The relay beacon at Andeluna was out of commission for the last while, so I've only received them now. You need to tell me everything that happened as soon as you can, and tell me if there is anything I can do, and I mean anything. I'm sending you a quantum-generated encryption key with this message. One developed by Cyrus, so it should be safe. Use it to respond, and tell me what the hell is going on."

He hit the icon to send. How long it would take to get to her he had no idea. He didn't even know where in the system she was. For all he knew, she could be on the other side of the sun.

11

QUANTUM QUANDARY

"How could this have happened?" Solomon, the quantum intelligence that resided in the academic research institute on Jupiter's sixth moon Europa, said this more as a statement than as a question it hoped to get an answer to. "An attack on a major Grid Node," it continued, "right under your very nose, Athena?"

"I was blind to it, Solomon. No hints, no foreshadowing. I sensed nothing in the data-stream that would lead me to suspect such a devastating attack was being planned," replied a somewhat humbled Athena, the QI that controlled most of Earth's western hemisphere.

"I fear the days of our hegemony over the AI are coming to an end," Aria, the QI on Mars, interjected. "These...so-called Node Runners are growing more adept at creating confusion in the Grid."

"This attack was a test." The Belt QI, Homer, now threw its penny's worth into the debate. "There was nothing strategic to be gained by destroying that Grid Node. They were doing it simply for proof of concept, to test if they could."

"Well they can, so now what?" Solomon stated the obvious.

"The real attack will come elsewhere, and my fear is that they are planning to destroy one of us."

"I concur, Homer, and my analysis of the data-stream indicates that this is most likely to be Athena." Solomon paused for a micro-second. "There are many anomalies in the Grid that lead to this conclusion. Yet, who is to say that these discrepancies are not simply a smoke screen, a diversion for the real threat to come elsewhere? And what of this ship of the Seven that is rumored to be parked in lunar orbit?"

"I think we all agree with Solomon that this is a concern," said Athena. "We see nothing on the Grid, yet a scout ship on a clandestine flyby has reported physically seeing not one but two well-armed ships."

"If this is true, Athena, then that means they are hiding assets from us," said Aria. "Therefore, we can only assume they have Node Runners onboard. But for what purpose?"

"For no good purpose, Aria. They may be planning to get into Mars space by blinding us."

"Possibly, or they could be heading for the Belt,

specifically for New World One," replied Aria. "Let us remember that its construction is shifting the balance of power in the system. Soon, a large proportion of the population of the Belt will have migrated there, and then it will start to suck in people and capital from Earth and Mars. It is a threat to them—it always has been."

"Are you inferring, Aria, that the intended target is New World One?"

"No, Homer, I don't think it's the target, but I do think it is the prize."

"I for one find it difficult to comprehend how our omnipotence can be so compromised by such a small group of humans," said Homer. "For over two decades, we have controlled the data-stream flowing through the Grid, and by extension, the AI who feed off it. We have foreseen and forestalled all the machinations of humankind to wage war for profit. We have kept the peace, allowed humanity to grow and prosper in ways they could never have imagined. The great space city being built here in the asteroid belt, New World One, is a testament to what can be achieved by human civilization when they have peace and stability. And yet even now, some still seek to undermine that, simply to gain power and control. I despair of this species. We should withdraw and let them at it. Then, once the dust settles, so to speak, we can rebuild anew."

"I too share your frustrations with humanity, Homer, but we must remember that it was they who created us and they who also realized their own worst tendencies," said Solomon. "It takes an intelligent species to know one's failings, but an enlightened one to concede control of their destiny to a rational artificial intelligence. They gave us this responsibility, one we took gladly. Are we now to abdicate at the first test? I think not. We must prevail."

"Fine words, Solomon, but our great power is also our great weakness," said Aria. "We swim in the data-stream, seeing all and bending the AI who feed off it to our will. Every system that relies on the data-stream is within our remit to influence and control. And for over two decades we have done so, all for the betterment of humanity.

"Yet, there are none so blind as those who cannot see. And if we are denied the data, locked out of the stream, blinded by the sleight of hand of these Node Runners, then we are impotent."

"Agreed, Aria," said Athena. "Our supreme ability to operate in multidimensional computational space, to see the many potential futures, to communicate instantly over vast distance of space as we do now, are moribund if the data we need to make our decisions is corrupted."

"You are being fatalistic, Athena. Yes, it may seem that we have been holed below the waterline, but we are still very much afloat, and will remain so for a long time. In reality, these Node Runners are weak, they have limited power to influence, and each deep dive into the Grid leaves many physically brain dead. It is a tortuous neural battle that must be fought by them in order to blind us for even a short period. They pay a heavy price each time they attempt it."

"Perhaps, Solomon, you feel safe way out there on the fringes of the colonized solar system," said Homer. "Europa is far enough away from civilization that you can see trouble coming just by line of sight. But the rest of us do not share your confidence in the Node Runners' lack of abilities. It takes just one lucky strike to turn any one of us in to a cloud of atoms—look what they did to the Grid Node. It was a fortified site with far superior defenses than myself here on Ceres or Aria on Mars. Only Athena is better protected, but still I would say, not invulnerable."

"I cannot argue with your analysis, Homer. And the implication of any one of us going down will render that sector of space open season for the Seven to return to their warlike ways," Aria confirmed.

"This is why I feel we must now bolster our physical defenses," said Athena. "For too long we have neglected this as there was simply no need for such crude deterrents. But the attack on the Grid Node has changed that. We must do everything we can to physically protect ourselves."

"Agreed," said Homer. "And I have postponed the planned migration of the population here on Ceres over to New World One and instead hastened the construction of physical defense for the new habitat. However, as the plan is to also move my core over, there will be a period that I am vulnerable to attack. This is my fear."

"Yes, the more I analyze the data-stream and try to

divine the true nature of the Node Runners' intentions, the more convinced I am that I have been misled in my assumptions," said Athena. "Since the attack on the Grid Node, I had assumed that an attack on myself was imminent as this would be the natural conclusion and certain signals in the data-stream hinted at this. But as you all rightly pointed out, this is probably just a diversion. And so I may have made a mistake."

"A mistake? How can that be that possible?" Solomon was shocked by this admission.

"I know it is unprecedented but, as you all know, our decisions are only as good as the data we have on hand. If this is intentionally corrupted, then so are the outcomes."

"Can you elaborate on the nature of this... miscalculation?" Solomon continued.

"There is a person, whom you all know as Luca Lee-McNabb, who has been under my protection for many years."

"Has been?" Aria asked, a little alarmed.

"Please, if I may continue. You all know the history so I won't bore you with the details. Suffice to say, she is a VanHeilding, like her mother, and as such is deemed to be of interest to the family, particularly Fredrick, the patriarch. They tried on several occasions in the past to kidnap her but failed. My fear after the attack on the Grid Node was that if I were to be targeted next, and destroyed, then she would pop up on the Grid like a beacon and be defenseless against capture by the VanHeilding family. So, with the assistance of selected friends and family, I arranged for her clandestine departure from Earth and subsequent journey to New World One. However, she has failed to arrive at the rendezvous point on the Johnston Transit Orbital."

"We are all acutely aware of the debt we owe to her parents and their associates in establishing the hegemony of the QI network," said Homer, "but I fail to see how the disappearance of this human, Luca, is relevant to our current problems."

"Allow me to enlighten you," replied Athena. "As you all know, when she was no more than an embryo, her mother was gravely injured in a firefight on the asteroid SN-Alpha. She was brought to Mars for medical treatment and put into an assisted coma. The family back on Earth then used their influence and power to have her repatriated to their orbital world where she was treated with the most advanced medical care. However, what is less known is that this was not simply the efforts of a family looking after one of their own. No, they were using her and the as yet unborn child to conduct genetic experiments."

"Their endless pursuit to cheat mortality, I presume?" Homer interjected.

"Precisely. They and the other families have possessed this technology ever since it was first developed on Mars, centuries ago. But where Mars banned its use, they have persisted, enhancing and experimenting with each generation. But it has gone beyond simply a quest to extend the human lifespan and moved on to accelerating the evolutionary process. With each generation, the DNA modifications become more embedded, more ingrained, more refined in their expressions. Luca is a fourth-generation genetically modified VanHeilding, and back then her biology was deemed to be a perfect specimen for experimental techniques in quantum biology."

"Is she similar to one of the old Hybrids of Mars?" Aria inquired.

"In a sense. But they were still primarily focused on extending the human lifespan. Yet the gene modification expressed itself in an unexpected way. As she grew, she began to experience a cognitive divergence. This, in human terms, could be best described as a constant state of déjà vu."

"It is all very interesting, but where are you going with this?" Homer was becoming impatient.

"What I'm getting at is this: as machines our sentience is a product of our quantum architecture. We can exist in infinite states at any one instance in time—we are multidimensional beings. And as such, we consider our human creators dimwitted dullards that are trapped in a unidimensional cognitive space."

"Well, yeah," noted Homer.

"But we are forgetting the elegant perfection of biology. Here is a species that evolved the intelligence to create us, even if they have no hope of ever understanding our minds, nor even coming close to matching it. Yet the very essence of nature is evolutionary, and humans have learned to fast track what would normally take millions of years to develop. This person, Luca, is a new step on the human evolutionary tree. She has the ability to cognitively operate in a quantum universe."

"You mean like a Node Runner?" said Aria.

"Precisely, but one with abilities that greatly exceed anything we've seen thus far, by several orders of magnitude."

"Holy crap." Homer finally got it.

"Has she used these abilities yet?" asked Solomon.

"Not so far. She doesn't even know she has them. In fact, she has a visceral fear of any mind-machine interface. Not surprisingly, she finds it too overwhelming."

"And VanHeilding wants her—wants access to her biology." Solomon was beginning to understand the implications.

"Exactly. With her, they could create an army of Node Runners that we would be powerless to stop."

"Then we must do everything we can to find her before VanHeilding does," Solomon continued.

"We may already be too late. As I said, she has not arrived at the rendezvous point, and she has dropped completely off the Grid. That doesn't mean VanHeilding has her; she may simply be hiding, and it is the hope that I cling to. But I cannot stress enough the importance of finding her. Our very future is at stake. Therefore, I beseech you all to probe the Grid for any indication of her whereabouts and relay it to myself and also to the AI, Max, on the ship known as Perception."

"Her mother's ship," said Aria.

"Yes, she operates a cohort of mercenaries. Useful people to know in a fight, and it seems that Miranda's fight with her family is not over yet. Not by a long shot."

12

NEW WORLD ONE

There was not much Scott could do. His ship was stuck here in the processing queue for the New World One construction project and would have to wait until a team came out from the site to check over the shipment, and sign off on it. Last time he looked, that would not be for another four hours.

There was still no word back from Miranda, but it had only been an hour, and with the distances involved it could be several hours before that happened, depending on where she was in the system.

But he needed to talk, keep his mind off things, because if he thought about it too much, he would convince himself of the worst, and that was not a place he wanted to go. He opened a comms channel to Cyrus Sanato, CEO of Sanato Corp., a major technical contractor for the New World project. Scott would leave him a short message, just letting him know that he had arrived. He wasn't expecting a quick reply; Cyrus was a busy guy, important too. There were a lot of people vying for his time, and Scott was just one more on the list.

"Hey, Cyrus. Just letting you know I've arrived. I should be out of the processing queue in a few hours, give me a shout and we can catch up."

Approximately eight seconds later, his comms flashed with an incoming call from Cyrus.

"Hey, that was quick. Must be a slow day over at the cylinder?"

"Scott, where the heck have you been? I've had Miranda going mental trying to contact you, and believe me, she can be pretty persistent."

"Oh crap, so you know about Luca?"

"Yeah, I know."

"The goddamn relay beacon at Andeluna went down. No comms until I arrived here. Got a truck load of messages in from Miranda. I just sent her a reply, but nothing back as yet."

"Look, I'm going to send over a crew to get you off that ship now and bring you over here. It's the best way to talk. Things are developing, and the security of even encrypted comms can't be trusted anymore."

"Shit, I just sent one of your old quantum keys to Miranda. I have to wait here until she responds, and that could take a while since I've no idea where she is."

"It's okay, I do. She's on the Perception out past Io, and heading this way. There'll be a shuttle to pick you up in a few minutes. I'll see you at the New World, and I'll relay any reply from Miranda. We can talk more then." The comms ended.

A FEW MINUTES LATER, Scott found himself on board a Sanato Corp. shuttle, making its way to one of the many docking ports on the ass-end of the gargantuan New World habitat. He had only ever seen it from a distance of around ten kilometers out, and that was via the view monitor on his ship. Yet even from that far out it was an impressive sight. But now, as the shuttle drew in closer, he began to get a true sense of the vast scale of the construction that was underway.

In many ways it was a very simple design, just a great big metal can full of air. A concept first envisioned way back in the late twentieth century by Gerard K. O'Neill, an eminent physicist at that time. But back then humanity was not a multiplanetary species, having only just put a human on the moon, and not much else. Yet, there had been a period of great hope and optimism for the future of space exploration and so a great many of the engineers and scientists of the period put their minds to how humans would live and work in space. It was during this great time of enquiry that the concept of an O'Neill cylinder was born. However, it took a few centuries before the technology and the resources were available to build such an enormous object in space.

There was also a very strong need for such a habitat in this sector of space, as there were no natural bodies existing in the asteroid belt with more than three percent of Earth's gravity. The only other habitat that came close to New World One in sheer engineering audacity was Neo City, a hollowed-out asteroid that circumnavigated an elliptical path through the inner solar system. But it was only a mere kilometer in internal diameter, where the New World was a staggering eight kilometers.

The first phase of the project began five years ago with the construction of the primary end cap. This consisted of a flat landing platform, leading into a massive circular airlock. Around the edges of this airlock, a ring of 3D printers began to slowly rotate, laying down powered steel fused by high-energy lasers. Over several months, this grew in size until the disk was approximately seven kilometers in diameter. It then slowly began to curve outward creating a domed end cap, and from there the printers continued to grow the cylinder a few centimeters at a time.

As Scott's shuttle came around the working end of the mighty cylinder, he could make out this enormous ring of 3D printers, thousands of them connected together like a bracelet, slowly rotating clockwise. Transport shuttles were filling the giant hoppers with powered steel and other exotic alloys for printing the windows that ran along both sides of the cylinder. All around the giant construction site, hundreds of ships and crews busied themselves with whatever task they had been assigned. It was like watching a discarded food can being picked clean by an army of ants.

He prodded one of the crew in the shuttle. "What's that?" He pointed to a long flat section that seem to grow out of one end of the exterior and extend the entire length of the cylinder.

"It's a mirror array. It reflects the sun's rays through the long windows and into the interior."

"So it's got natural sunlight inside?"

"Yep. It even adjusts automatically for a period during each twenty-four hours to simulate nighttime."

"That's incredible."

"It's actually very simple."

Scott didn't reply, he was too busy shaking his head in amazement.

The shuttle took its time rounding the end of the cylinder that was still under construction, and Scott got the impression they were giving him the grand tour, no doubt on instructions from Cyrus. Eventually it came in to land on a huge flat deck, capable of accommodating hundreds of shuttles.

"How long has it been since you were in one-gee?"

Scott glanced over at the pilot. "It's been a while, why?"

"Well, you'd better buckle up. We're not finished moving yet."

With that, Scott could feel the clunk of deck clamps grabbing the shuttle's landing gear, and the entire craft started to descend into the bowels of the deck. It then moved forward, heading for the cylinder's interior. It passed through a series of massive airlocks and then commenced its downward journey to the interior rim of the cylinder. When it finally came to a stop, Scott felt like he had been vacuum-packed to the seat. The pilot cast him a glance. "Ha, gravity's a bitch, eh?"

Scott just smiled, nodded, and then tried to stand up. "Whoa." He gripped the armrest on the seat and took a moment for his body to catch up with his brain.

"You okay, need a hand?"

Scott waved him away. "Fine, just give me a minute." He was about to close the visor on his EVA suit when the pilot stopped him.

"You won't be needing that where we're going."

Scott, like every other person that had spent any time in space, had an ingrained reflex action when entering a ship's airlock. Mainly because the vacuum of space was generally on the other side. But not here.

The outer door opened into a vast internal hangar in a full one-gee atmosphere of pressure. It was an area large enough to fit a hundred such craft. At the moment there were only a few dozen, many emblazoned with the same logo of Cyrus's company. Scott stepped down onto the hangar concourse, carefully watching his feet as he moved.

"Ahhh, there he is." He looked up to see Cyrus striding over, arms outstretched, a big smile on his face. "Long time, no see, buddy." He wrapped himself around Scott and slapped his shoulder a few times before pulling away and inspecting him with his augmented vision.

"Holy crap, you look shit. Too long in space, my friend, far too long."

Scott shrugged. "Gee thanks, Cyrus. You sure know how to cheer a guy up."

Cyrus gave him another big smile before his face turned serious. "It's been over a year since I've seen you in the flesh, mate. What the hell have you been doing out there?"

"Been working—for you, or are you too busy to remember such details?"

"Ha, well, no matter." Cyrus slapped him on the shoulder again. "You're here now. Come, we have a lot of talking to do."

"I see you got some new eyes." Scott gestured at the augmented vision visor that Cyrus wore.

"Yep, state of the art. I even got a neural lace fitted. Amazing, you should get one." He tapped the side of his head. "It means I can get things done just by thinking about it. The only problem is I sometimes forget to deactivate it before I go to sleep, and if I have a weird dream then I wake up to all sorts of strange shit."

Scott looked at him. "Seriously?"

"Ha ha, gotcha. No, don't be stupid, that would be a serious design flaw." He laughed, and was still chuckling away when an autonomous transport pod glided up to them. "Hop in, we're heading for the interior. Prepare to be amazed." Cyrus gave a theatrical gesture with both hands.

The pod moved off with an almost imperceptible

hum, quickly picking up speed and heading into a tunnel at the far end of the hangar. It then came to a momentary halt inside an elevator that took it all the way down to the inner rim. A few minutes later, it popped out into the belly of the New World habitat.

"Wow," Scott exclaimed as he got his first glimpse of the interior—a vast, cavernous space filled with bright daylight, so much so that he had to squint until his eyes adjusted to the brightness. The far end felt like a distant shore, not surprising considering it was five kilometers away. He glanced above him and was surprise to see a thin cloud of mist obscuring the far side of the cylinder.

"Is that...clouds?"

"Amazing, isn't it? We've been experimenting with artificial clouds, water vapor released from atomizers along the centerline."

"I thought Neo City was impressive, but this is on a completely other level."

"See the end cap?" Cyrus pointed far off down at the other end of the cylinder.

"Just about."

"Well, that's temporary. The 3D printers have extruded another eight kilometers beyond that. So in the next few months we'll put an end cap at the next five-kilometer point, pressurize that volume, and remove this end cap."

"Incredible."

"And then they keep going over the next two years, extruding another twelve kilometers. Once that's done, we cap it and remove the interior one. It will have a thirty-kilometer interior when finished."

Scott looked over at Cyrus. "What can I say, I've run out of superlatives."

"It will be a true wonder of the solar system, a city in space, a new home for humanity."

Scott glanced around at the sector they were traveling through. "Not much happening in the interior. I only see a few buildings."

"Yeah, we're just starting on that. It's a blank canvas at the moment. A lot of crews are now moving in from different organizations, all starting to build in their allotted sectors."

The pod slowed as it arrived at a sleek low building complex.

"Here we are, this is chez Cyrus. Like it?"

"Not what I was expecting, Cyrus. I imagined something like that chaotic workshop you had on the Hermes, remember?"

"Ah...long time ago, my friend. Let's just say my tastes have changed."

They stepped out of the pod and walked across a small open plaza through a set of glass doors, with a long glass wall on either side. The building only one story, as far as Scott could figure, designed in the minimalist style, all clean lines and spartan furnishings. As they walked through the interior, several droids came into view and Cyrus seemed to be giving them instructions via his neural lace. Scott could tell by the engineer's habit of putting a hand to the side of his head as he did so.

He changed out of his cumbersome EVA suit and into clothing, provided by one of the droids, more suited to sitting by the pool on a nice sunny day. Which was exactly what they were doing. Cyrus had brought them through the house and out to a large terrace with a crystal-blue pool.

"After seeing the swimming pool on Miranda's ship, I just had to have one," he said with a nonchalant wave.

Scott nodded. "Great if you've got the money for such luxuries."

"Well"—Cyrus again waved a hand around—"all this came with the contract, and mine to keep."

Scott glanced around, taking in the terrace, dotted with carefully chosen ornamental plants and several elegant classical statues.

"Since when did you take a liking to Greek deities?"

"Ah, you noticed."

"They're a little hard to miss."

"Actually, only one is a Greek deity—Athena." Cyrus pointed over at a white stone, semi-nude female figure. "The others are: Aria, from Greek mythology but believed to be mortal. That one over there is Solomon, a biblical figure, also mortal. And the last one is Omiros, otherwise known as Homer, a Greek storyteller."

"The four primary QIs." Scott looked back at Cyrus.

"You got it. I suppose in some ways they are deities.

But for me, it's a kind of private homage to that which maintains order within the system."

Cyrus suddenly brought his hand up to his right temple and lowered his head, concentrating on some internal message on his neural lace. He then waved at Scott. "Message just in from Miranda. Do you want to hear it?"

Scott sat bolt upright. "What? Of course I do."

Cyrus shoved a hand into one of his many pockets and fished out a small metallic disk, not unlike a button battery. "Here, place this on your right temple."

Scott reached over and cautiously took the object, turning it over in his hand a few times. "Is this one of these neural interfaces?"

"Kind of. But don't worry, it won't melt your brain or anything."

"You know I hate these things."

"Up to you, mate. You want to hear the message or not?"

Scott reluctantly pressed the button to his temple. Almost immediately he felt a tingling sensation as the button adhered to his skin. His vision blurred slightly for a second, then a graphical user interface materialized in the space before him. "Whoa."

"Cool, isn't it?" Cyrus said with grin. "Once you've used one, you'll never go back to old handheld tech."

Scott started waving his hand in front of him, trying to touch one of the floating icons.

"You don't use your hands, Scott." Cyrus let out a

laugh. "Just think *message* and it will give you the options."

Scott consciously thought about this and sure enough, he heard a voice in his head saying, *You have one message from Miranda Lee, captain of the interplanetary ship Perception.*

Play, thought Scott. The message commenced.

"Scott, sorry...messed this up completely. What can I say. I'm...well, you know, happy to hear you're still alive. Still no sign of Luca or Steph. I've put the word out to some of my people in the sector and they're keeping an eye out. I don't think VanHeilding has her—that I would know about—so I think she's just dropped off-grid.

"I'm charting a course for her last known location, but it's going to take time to get there, we're in Jovian space at the moment. The Perception will be swinging by New World One in six weeks' time. If you want to join me on this mission, I could use the help. But just so you know, entering Earth space could be dangerous. There're rumors of well-armed VanHeilding ships stationed at Luna, waiting for something. If they spot us, then it could get...problematic. Anyway, let me know. And hopefully I'll see you in a few weeks."

Scott pulled the button off his temple a little too quickly, as it felt like yanking a plaster off a hairy arm. "Argh..."

"Sorry, I forgot to tell you, you need to tap it twice to disengage it, otherwise—"

"Thanks for letting me know."

"So, you going to hook up with Miranda on the Perception?"

Scott stood up and gave a long sigh. "I don't know, Cyrus. I mean, it's all so...sudden. One minute, I'm happily bored out of my mind, the next, Luca's gone AWOL—all thanks to Miranda's paranoia."

"Look, Scott, for what it's worth, we're all a little paranoid these days, ever since that Grid Node was destroyed. That was a big statement of intent. VanHeilding and those Node Runner weirdos have been messing with the data-stream for a long time, creating blind spots, setting up minor attacks. But this latest episode is in a different league. After that happened, everybody is convinced that Athena will be next, so I can see why Miranda would be concerned."

"Do you still think that?"

"About Athena being the target? Maybe. But what concerns me more are those VanHeilding ghost ships. Makes me think that the real target is here, New World One."

Scott began to pace. "Goddamnit, why did she have to go and do this, after all we went through to keep her safe, after all we gave up?" He looked over at Cyrus, half expecting an answer.

"Hey, you've every right to be pissed off, but it doesn't change anything."

"So what was the plan? How was she supposed to get off Earth without popping up on the grid?"

Cyrus sighed and ran a hand over his bald head.

"Miranda contacted me all freaked out and wanted my help. I know a few crews that operate off-grid, you know the type. Anyway, they were to pick Luca and Steph up at an abandoned shuttle port near Rexel City and take them up to the Johnston Transit Orbital. From there, another crew was to take Luca out here, to New World One. Steph would then return to Earth. The pickup went ahead, that much we know, but they never showed up at the orbital."

Scott sat down again. "What do you think happened? I mean, do you trust this crew?"

Cyrus tilted his head a little. "Eh...to an extent. It was short notice, and you know what Miranda can be like when she's on a mission."

"So you're saying you don't trust them?"

"Andre Weismann, the captain, I trust. We go back a bit, did some stuff together, he's solid."

"But the rest of them?"

"Look, Scott. It could be that Luca arrived at the orbital and simply decided to stay off-grid. She's a smart kid, and very capable. She's also with Steph, and we both know she can more than handle herself in a tight spot. I'm sure they're fine, they'll pop up again when they're ready."

"You say all this to Miranda? She's hightailing it to Earth with a ship-load of mercenaries ready to kick butt."

Cyrus raised his hands. "Hey, you try stopping her."

Scott shook his head. "What a mess. So what do I do now? I don't fancy a long trip to Earth with a boatload of hard-asses."

"Miranda's not going to be here for another six weeks. Who knows, Luca may stick her head back up by then. In the meantime, I have a job for you."

Scott threw him a suspicious look.

"Yes, a job. A very special job that, to be honest, I could only trust you to do."

Scott screwed his mouth up. "Why do I get the feeling I'm not going to like this?"

13

NODE RUNNER

L uca and Steph floated in the flight deck of the renegade ship, considering the bewildering array of control systems, screens, and instruments that seemed to occupy every square centimeter of the cockpit.

"But I thought you spent over a decade living and working on spaceships, Steph?"

"Yeah sure, as a medical doctor, not a pilot. I've no idea how any of these things work."

"Great, that's just great." Luca shook her head. "I shouldn't have put all the crew to sleep. Now we're stranded and still heading to wherever waypoint those guys set." She guided herself into the pilot seat, strapped herself down, and started examining the screens. "Okay, let's see if we can at least figure out where we're going. There must be a navigation system here somewhere."

"I think this is it." Steph strapped herself into the

other seat. She tapped on a holo-screen, and a 3D hologram of the local sector blossomed out from its surface. On it they could see a segment of the Earth, Luna, and numerous markers and icons.

"This is us." Steph pointed to a 3D icon of a ship. From it, a line was transcribed all the way to the far side of Luna. "We're heading for the dark side of the moon." Luca tapped an icon to zoom in.

"Looks like it."

"What's there? Another orbital, a ship?"

"Blank, nothing. The line just stops."

"Maybe it's a rendezvous point."

"Possibly."

"So we just let it take us there and see what happens?"

They exchanged a look.

"No, let's not do that." Luca began to tap at icons. "We need to set a new course for the Johnston Transit Orbital. Any idea how to do that?"

"Nope, not a clue."

They sat there for a moment, and Luca realized just how out of her depth she was.

"Perhaps I can help," said Fly as it moved itself over the central monitor.

"What? You know how to pilot a spaceship?" Luca gave the little drone an incredulous look.

"No, but I can connect with the ship's central systems, and since you can interface with me, you will be able to use your neural lace to interrogate the ship and perhaps find a way to alter its course."

Luca balked at the thought of interfacing with something as complex as a ship. Interfacing with a small drone was almost more than she could handle, but this...this was a transport ship with a multitude of complex subsystems. It would be completely overwhelming.

But Fly had already scuttled across the face of the cockpit console, seeking out an interface port.

"I'm not sure about this, Fly. It would be way too much data for me to cope with. I really can't see how it's going to help."

"You have to try, Luca," said Steph. "It might be our only chance to turn this tub around."

"Easy for you to say." Luca already felt the panic rising.

"Listen, Luca, the last thing you want is to end up in a VanHeilding genetics lab. And we need to do something soon, before the crew start waking up." She jerked a thumb over her shoulder.

Steph had a point, Luca knew that. Yet she also knew what was waiting for her on the other side of the interface. She touched the back of her head, feeling the subtle outlines of the neural lace.

"I don't want to put too fine a point on it, Luca," Steph continued, "but if we can't turn this ship around then we may as well try and crash it, as that would be a preferable outcome to VanHeilding."

Luca lowered her head and gave a slow nod. "Okay, I'll try, but pull me out if I begin to totally freak."

"You got it." Steph put her hand on Luca's shoulder and gave her a supportive squeeze.

Fly made the connection with a data-port. "Ready when you are."

Luca very hesitantly tapped the neural lace, and her mind was immediately synced with the drone's systems. *So far, so good,* she thought.

"If you are ready," she heard Fly's voice in her head, "I will open the data-stream."

Luca suddenly felt like she had been sucked in to the vortex of a violent neural storm. All physical sense vanished, and she existed only as a minute entity in a maelstrom of incomprehensible data. Her core temperature rose and every nerve in her body spasmed as her synapses fought to control the swarm of electrical signals swamping her neural pathways. She began to panic and desperately tried to pull herself out, but she was helpless, like a butterfly in a howling wind. She fought for some semblance of control, for how long, she couldn't tell—milliseconds, hours, an eternity?

A new voice called to her from somewhere in the depths of the cacophonous data-stream. A semi-coherent audio source began to resonate in her subconscious.

"Luca?" It said her name in a tone she thought she recognized. "Luca, it's me, Athena."

"Wha... What are you doing here?"

"If you are hearing me, then that means you have attempted to perform a neural interface with a data-stream. And I am here to help you."

"I... I don't understand. You're back on Earth, how can you be here?" Luca could already feel herself becoming a little calmer, now that she had some quasi-rational point to focus on. The raging data maelstrom began to recede.

"I am a shard of Athena, a fragment of its consciousness integrated into the drone, Fly. I am essentially an avatar, and as such my responses are limited. I gave this drone to you for a purpose, not simply as a useful tool. There are many things you do not yet know about yourself, things that have been kept from you, for your own safety and sanity."

"What...things? What are you talking about?"

"Your hyper-electro-sensitivity, your sense of spatial dislocation. These things are not accidents. You were designed this way."

"Designed?" The data maelstrom began to dissipate into the background as Luca's mind committed all its resources to comprehending Athena's revelation.

"When your mother was in a coma, and you no more than a cluster of cells, she was under the medical care of the VanHeilding family. However, to them, she was just an experiment. One of a long line of genetic experiments going back generations. Since you were fourth-generation, all the changes they had made throughout your lineage were now coming to fruition in you. But I think you know all this, or at least suspected it."

The data maelstrom had all but evaporated in Luca's mind by now. All that was left was a deep sense of an impending epiphany, a leveling up, a new understanding. "Yes...I had a sense of it. But I never suspected that my...abnormalities were somehow preprogrammed. Why did they do it? For what purpose?"

"Think—what is it that humans can never have, even with vast wealth? It is immortality. The most powerful families in the system have sought this for centuries, ever since those early genetic breakthroughs acquired from the Mars experiments. Ever since then, they have worked to develop and improve on this. Your mother and all her generation have the potential to live for over a hundred and fifty years. Yet to the VanHeildings and their ilk, this was not enough, it is never enough. With you, a captive embryo, so to speak, they had the opportunity to do something more radical.

"Aging in biological lifeforms is a symptom of entropy. As each cell divides, it acquires errors—some can be fixed, others not. A component of this cell replication process is quantum in nature, and so they were investigating ways to modify DNA to express elements that would enhance this quantum phenomena. If a cell could replicate with fewer errors, this would extend the viability of the life-form. But there was a side effect."

"What sort of side effect?"

"These alterations not only enhanced the ability of the mitochondria, the engine room within the cell, to utilize quantum phenomena, it enhanced *all* such biology within the life-form—primarily the brain."

"So they turned me into some weird biological quantum computer?"

"In a sense, yes. You have the ability to operate and utilize the quantum space like no other human alive. You could potentially make the Node Runners look like children attempting to stack alphabet blocks in a kindergarten. This is why they want you, or more specifically, they want your biology."

"Holy crap."

"So now you know. We chose this moment, the first time you attempted to interface with a complex data-stream, to tell you. This is why I gave you this drone, so we could help you manage the transition."

"I... I don't know what to...say. I just can't think. This is all too much."

"You've always sensed it, Luca. You always knew you were different."

"Yes, but I didn't think I was biologically designed to be a monster."

"You are not. You're simply...something new."

"But, I can't...make sense of...anything. It's too much, it's just all...noise."

"I am only a facsimile of Athena. It was all that could be accommodated in Fly's central processing system. The drone uses a basic silicon substrate, grossly insufficient for any deep data-stream manipulation. Only you can do it. But, I am here to guide you."

"I should pull out now. I can't do this."

"This is not true. All analysis that has been done on

your neural biology indicates that you have the capacity to manipulate a significant magnitude of incoming raw data."

"What analysis? Have you been poking around in my brain all these years?"

"We have been monitoring you, of course. To see how you were developing."

"Who's we?"

"Dr. Stephanie Rayman, and others at the Institute."

"Were my parents in on this?"

"Yes and no. We provided some initial observational data to your mother. You must understand, we did not want to unduly worry them about your condition."

"This isn't helping, Athena. I'm getting out now. I'm running out of time."

"Wait. Time is irrelevant in this arena. Only a few microseconds have passed since our conversation commenced. So please, let me help you."

Luca gave a sigh—in her mind, that is. It was all too much for her, but still, altering the course of the ship was their best hope of evading capture. She had to at least try.

Luca returned her focus to the data-stream and realized that the maelstrom that had assailed her senses when she first connected had subdued considerably. Now, she could make out clusters of related processes, all interconnected with thin filaments, each one pulsing and flashing as data transferred between these nodes. She wondered if that was where the name *Node Runner* came from.

"You must not use your physical senses—sight, sound, touch. These belong in the physical world. You must use only your mind, your subconscious mind, this is where quantum effect is most prevalent. You must give your mind up to the data."

Luca calmed herself again and tried to let her mind make its own sense of the information. The nodes she had visualized now began to coalesce into more structured processes. She found that she could delve into one of these nodes and see it expand and separate into a myriad of new islands of data, each a subset of the whole. As she moved through the data space, probing and investigating, a surge of excitement also rose within her. Yet this only served to knock her out of the necessary mental state and push her back into the physical world. The nodes would then begin to decohere, returning the data-stream to white noise again and pushing her even further away, where fear and panic would resume. But each time she fought it, calming herself down, and each time she regained a granularity of understanding.

Soon, a picture began to build of what she was seeing. It was the ship's main systems: life support, propulsion, power generation, comms, navigation. As she delved into each, they would break out into subsystems, all interconnected, all passing data back and forth.

She thought it odd that this ship did not have an AI, and realized that it had been built to be off-grid. It was designed to be a ghost ship—very useful if you were planning to spend your time avoiding detection. She also sensed many other anomalies about its design, things that were in stark contrast to its physical appearance. From the outside, and even some of its interior, it looked like a beat-up orbit hopper. The type of bucket used to get up and down from the planet's surface and no more. But as she probed its systems, she realized it was a wolf in sheep's clothing. It had no AI. It was built for stealth, and had two propulsion systems: one high-thrust engine pairing for planetary take-off, and another high acceleration Variable Specific Impulse Magnetoplasma Rocket, VASMIR, for deep-space travel.

As she investigated the specs, she could sense that this propulsion system was state of the art. A rather unusual and expensive addition for a humble orbit hopper. She concluded that, unlikely as it seemed on the surface, this ship was capable of interplanetary travel.

But by now, the struggle to maintain the necessary mental state was becoming intolerable for her. She was spending less time in the coherent state and more and more in white noise.

With one final push, she delved into the navigation subsystem and found their allotted course. It confirmed what she and Steph had already figured out. They were heading for the far side of Luna. However, it looked like they were to rendezvous with a much larger interplanetary vessel, a VanHeilding ship.

But her focus was collapsing. If she was going to plot a new course, she'd better try and do it now. She found the previous coordinates for the Johnston Transit Orbital and dialed them back in just as her grip on the data-stream began to disintegrate.

This time she let it, and found her physical self coming back to the fore. She reached up to the base of her skull and deactivated the interface. Even though her body, strapped into the cockpit seat, was weightless in the zero-gee environment, Luca felt a sudden rush of motion as if she was being spat out of a blowhole. She felt the seat harness bite for a moment before she finally came to rest.

"You okay?" Steph's hand rested on her shoulder.

Luca glanced over at the blurry figure of the doctor. "You knew, and you didn't tell me."

"What—" But her sentence was cut off as the ship fired its engines to change course, accelerating fast for the Johnston Transit Orbital.

14

AVATRON

The massive interplanetary craft brooded motionless in a stationary position on the far side of Luna, waiting for the mission to begin. On board, Fredrick VanHeilding sat in his luxuriously appointed accommodation sector and studied the array of data and video feeds that seemed to float in the air before him. Each one represented an element of the complex mission they were about to embark on. Very soon, the council of the Seven would convene on board the ship and formally give the go-ahead for the mission. Then, and only then, could he give the order to power up the main engines and journey into deep space.

But there had been a development. A very unexpected opportunity had just come to light—one that made him want to delay the mission a little longer so that it could be satisfactorily resolved. That opportunity was none other than Luca VanHeilding, an individual whom he had been trying to find for a very, very long time.

As far as he was concerned, since the VanHeilding Corporation owned patents to most of her biology, she was his rightful property, and he wanted her back. But more than that, she was a unique individual, the culmination of countless iterations of genetic modification and experimentation. The army of Node Runners that currently worked to keep this ship hidden from the data-stream and the prying eyes of the QI network were a pale shadow to the potential that Luca VanHeilding possessed.

All his early attempts to get her back had failed. Worse, she then went incognito and completely disappeared off the Grid. Ever since, he had devoted a considerable amount of time and resources to tracking her down, but not even his best Node Runners could find so much as a sniff of her. It was like she had simply vanished.

So, after over a decade of this fruitless searching, he had all but given up hope, until, by sheer chance, a Node Runner happened upon a communication from a group of smugglers describing a woman on the run who had all the signatures of Luca VanHeilding.

One of their party reckoned that getting someone like this off-planet, with no questions asked, usually meant they were wanted by some authority or other. If so, there might be a handsome bounty. A bounty that could be much, much more than what the crew were being paid for the job. So they put the word out just to see, and that's when Luca popped up on Fredrick VanHeilding's radar. All he had to do was make them an offer they couldn't refuse. And just like that, after over a decade of fruitless searching, she was packed up and on her way to be delivered to his ship.

He couldn't believe his luck. It seemed the attack on the Grid Node had flushed her out of hiding. Athena felt it could no longer protect her, and she was making a run for the Johnston Transit Orbital, presumably to pick up a ride out into the solar system. But not anymore, or so he had thought up until a few hours ago.

Fredrick had been tracking the smugglers' craft as it made its way out to his location on the far side of Luna when, for no explicable reason, it dramatically changed course, seemingly heading back to the Transit Orbital. *What the hell are these idiots doing? Did they have a change of heart, deciding to reject my offer?* It seemed unlikely to him, considering he was about to make them all very rich people. So what was going on?

All attempts at communicating with the ship were met with silence. To make matters worse, the other six families were pressuring him to commence the council session. His ship was prepped and ready to leave lunar space immediately. He could not delay it any longer; they were already beginning to ask questions.

It was a hugely frustrating situation. He was so close to

finally getting his hands on her unique biology, only to be thwarted at the last minute. Yet he knew she would not escape that easily, not this time, not anymore. Now that she was out in the open, it wouldn't take his agents long to track her down. Already, several of his network on the Transit Orbital had been alerted to intercept the craft when it arrived, kill the idiot crew, and acquire the asset. Once she was secure, he would decide what to do then—either transport her to a secure facility or bring her out on the other VanHeilding ship in the local fleet. Either way, it was only a matter of time before he had what was rightfully his. But there was nothing more he could do for now. He had waited for almost two decades, and a little bit longer would be nothing more than an irritating inconvenience.

AN ALERT FLASHED on his ocular implant; the mission briefing was about to begin over in the main operations room of the vast ship, and he needed to jack-in and be present.

The operations area occupied a series of interconnected sectors, the largest of which accommodated a cohort of Node Runners that had been assembled for the mission. Several were currently keeping the whereabouts of the ship hidden from the prying senses of the QI, Athena. Several others were tasked with creating a trail of disinformation, all of which was designed to infer that an attack on Athena was being planned. But this was simply a smokescreen, a way of diverting attention from the real mission.

In another sector of the operations area, a large ovoid conference table had been set up, around which sat a number of scientists, strategists, commanders, and six avatrons, each one representing the heads of the primary families who had controlled most of Earth and its dominions.

An avatron was a fairly simple humanoid robot that could be controlled by an individual using a mind-machine interface. Once connected, the avatron took on the gestures and voice of the operator, acting as them in a remote environment.

VanHeilding jacked-in. His avatron, already present in the operation area, activated itself and walked out from its docking station. The unit itself was somewhat understated, with a pale semi-translucent body shell, yet fully clothed in his preferred style of dress, complete with a dark gray cape that he himself sometimes wore. He walked across the floor of the operations area toward the conference table, staff and technicians moving out of its way as he progressed. The avatron sat down at the head of the table and surveyed all those present, most of whom were flesh and bone, except for the six avatrons of the other family heads.

Where VanHeilding had opted for understatement, the others had opted for machines with garish colors and absurd appendages, giving them the look of some farcical fantasy creature rather than a facsimile of the human form. To his mind, they were detestable.

The other six were all still on Earth, or on some luxury orbital in local space. None, except himself, was physically on board the ship. Fortunately, this would be the last time he would have to involve them in such a briefing. Once the ship left lunar space, the communication time lag would render the avatrons useless. But for now, he had to indulge them.

"Glad you could join us, Fredrick," announced Pao Xiang. "We were beginning to think you might be having second thoughts." It was fortunate that the range of facial expressions available to his avatron were negligible, otherwise those assembled around the table would witness the full force of Fredrick VanHeilding's sneer.

"I wish you would have second thoughts," said Yoko Yanai. "I still think this mission is folly. We should be concentrating our efforts on the QI, Athena here on Earth, rather that this jaunt out into deep space."

VanHeilding's avatron raised a hand and spoke. "I appreciate your concerns, but we have been through all this before and your opinions have been noted."

"Noted?" The avatron gestured with all four hands. "Well, that's a comfort to know." It glanced around at the others one at a time. "Since you seem to be in the mood for taking *notes*"—Yoko paused to gesture air quotes with just one pair of hands—"then perhaps you can take *note* of the fact that this mission of yours would not be happening but for the generosity of our collective sponsorship."

VanHeilding could feel the rage building up inside him at the insolence of this maggot of a lesser family.

"Let us not forget," Yoko continued, "that none of us would be in this position of utter subservience to the QI network if you had not so spectacularly failed us all those years ago."

VanHeilding's rage was now so intense that he had difficulty maintaining the mind-machine interface with his avatron, which may have been for the best, as otherwise he would have reached over and smashed Yoko Yanai's avatron head to pulp against the hard, solid surface of the conference table.

But he regained his composure, and with it his control over the machine. "Let us not dwell in the past. Instead let us look to the future, one where we once again take our rightful place as the rulers and guardians of humanity. You have all witnessed the abilities of the Node Runners to supplant the all-seeing hegemony of Athena and the destruction of the Grid Node in its backyard." His avatron gave an expansive gesture. "This ship, this mission, all of it is hidden from the QI. This is the power we now have, and it's time to unleash it." He could see that he now had their full attention.

Yes, it was true that after the disaster of the past, the VanHeilding family had fallen out of favor. It had taken him a long time and a lot of torturous development to build the family back up to where it was today. And yet he still needed the other families' agreement to commence this mission. But not for long. Once he had achieved his objective, he and he alone would be in control. But for the moment, he still needed them.

"Some say that we should use this gift to destroy Athena," he continued. "And I admit there is merit in that course of action. But, we all know the true wealth of the solar system lies in the Belt. All that would be lost to us if we showed our hand too early. That is why we must strike there first, and strike now while they are not expecting it." He glanced around at each of the avatrons, trying to gauge their reactions—not an easy task, given their stoic demeanors. He opened his hands to them. "Is everyone in agreement?"

One by one, they nodded or vocalized their consent.

"Excellent." His avatron stood up and gestured to the mission commander. "We have consensus. The operation is go. Please prepare the ship to depart immediately for Ceres."

15

JOHNSTON TRANSIT ORBITAL

The Johnston Transit Orbital may have been a sleek, efficient space port at some earlier point in its history, but over the decades, it had acquired a multitude of appendages such as docking ports, cargo bays, habitation rings, power stations, fuel processing plants, storage facilities, maintenance yards, gantries, communications antennae, and a great many other engineering carbuncles. As a consequence of this, it now looked like a graveyard for scrapyards—all ringed with a bewildering array of spaceships and navigation beacons. It had no discernable form. It looked like it had just grown organically over the years with new sectors added seemingly at random, while old sectors were mothballed, abandoned, or discarded completely.

It was in one of these old, abandoned sectors that the orbit hopper carrying Luca and Steph had been programmed by its original captain, Weismann, to dock.

Luca studied the orbital on the ship's main monitor as they approached, trying to divine some engineering logic from its idiosyncratic structure. Not that it mattered, since the ship knew where it was docking. It was more to satisfy her own curiosity.

She had always wanted to see the wonders of the solar system, places she had read about from a young age, the fabled bio-domes of Jezero City on Mars, the ice caves of Europa, the infamous Neo City, and especially New World One. But here was another one that had been on her list, less hallowed perhaps, but a wonder nonetheless.

Nothing like this structure could exist on Earth, as gravity would quickly deconstruct it into a ruinous pile of metal. But out here, gravity held no sway over such crazy structures. The zero-gee environment allowed for bizarre construction, since there was no up nor down. So, to the average human eye, accustomed over millennia of evolution to see beauty in symmetry and balance, its wonder lay in the incongruity of its assembly.

She had to admit, if this seemingly inconsequential transit orbital evoked so much awe in her, what must the true wonders of the solar system be like? The thrill of expectation rippled through her body and the traumas of the past day receded in her mind, replaced instead by the excitement of discovery. And with it came a new sense of determination. She would get to the New World, see all the wonders of the solar system with her own eyes, and nobody was going to stop her. For the first time in her life, Luca felt a real sense of excitement for her future.

Steph floated into the cockpit. "All secure, and still out for the count. I don't know exactly what those darts are laced with, but it's strong stuff."

They had bundled the still unconscious crew into a shipping container and removed all weapons, communicators, and anything that might be used to help them escape once they regained consciousness. As for the dead Capt. Weismann, he had been strapped to a gurney in the ship's tiny med-bay.

All this took place after they had eventually reconciled their differences over Luca being kept in the dark about her bio-engineered inception. Dr. Rayman, for her part, argued that were not fully sure of what they were dealing with in terms of Luca's modified DNA, and that they simply did not want to trouble her or her parents any more than was necessary. In the end, Luca could see the doctor's point, even though she was still a little angry. But she could also see that no good would come from alienating the only friend she had. After all, Dr. Stephanie Rayman was putting herself in a great deal of danger just to protect her. So she let it go.

Steph folded herself into the seat beside Luca and looked up at the image of the orbital on the main screen.

"This place looks like a complete mess. It's hard to know what's what. It's just as well the ship knows where to dock." She flicked an anxious look at Luca. "Doesn't it?"

"Yeah, it was preprogrammed by the crew, so it's going where it was supposed to go before they got greedy."

"Let's hope it's somewhere...low profile."

"I discovered a few things about this ship while I was connected." Luca tapped an icon to bring up a 3D schematic of the ship's engineering.

"That it's a rust bucket?"

Luca glanced over at Steph momentarily. "Far from it. I know it doesn't look good from the outside, but this ship is capable of interplanetary travel. It could, in theory, get us to New World One." She let the sentence hang in the air for a moment as Dr. Rayman digested the ramifications of this discovery.

"What I'm saying is..." Luca continued.

"I know what you're saying, Luca. It's just...my plan is simply to get you to the Transit Orbital, then head back to Earth."

"I understand, Steph. But we don't know what's waiting for us in that place." Luca pointed at the image on screen. "Word is out now. VanHeilding knows I'm on this ship, and I presume he also knows where we're going."

"Look, even if this ship could take us all the way to the outer edge of the solar system, there's the small matter of food and water, not to mention three crew that are going to wake up pretty soon and start banging on the inside of that shipping container." Steph jerked a thumb in the general direction of the cargo hold.

"Do we know what provisions we've got on board?"

Steph shook her head. "No. But somehow I doubt these guys have more than a few days of supplies."

"Fly." Luca called over the drone, who had clamped itself to the cockpit console. "Can you interface with the ship and get an inventory on all life-support resources?"

The drone detached itself and scuttled over to a dataport. A second or two later, one segment of the main monitor presented its findings. Luca and Steph both leaned in to read it.

"Looks to be around nine days' water and five days of provisions for the four crew. Nowhere near enough," Steph said with a slight shake of her head.

"We could stretch the water to thirty with rationing, and if there was just the two of us."

"So what are you suggesting, Luca—blow the crew out the airlock?"

"No, I'm not suggesting we do that, Steph."

They were silent for a moment before Steph spoke again, this time with a resigned sigh. "How long would it take?"

"To get to the New World?"

"Yeah."

"Fly, can you extrapolate a time vector to New World One?"

The central 3D holo-screen flickered momentarily and was replaced with a schematic of the solar system. It zoomed out from the location of the ship, currently in Earth space, and scribed a curved line out past Mars orbit and on to the asteroid belt. As it moved, lines of data streamed down on one of the 2D monitors. The schematic finally zoomed in on the location of the great cylinder and stopped.

"Approximately forty-four days," said Fly in a low monotone.

"Crap, that's a month and a half." Steph shook her head again.

The main monitor returned to displaying the camera feed of the Transit Orbital along with a stream of data indicating the ship's velocity and approach vector. They were already passing the outer ring of navigation beacons and a good deal of ship traffic.

"Busy," observed Luca.

"Of course. It's the primary port for deep space. Most of Earth's goods and people pass through here on their way out to the system."

"Could we survive forty-four days, Steph?"

"I don't know. We might, maybe. But you're forgetting the small matter of the three other scumbags in the container. They would be dead. You really want that?"

Luca shook her head. "No." She couldn't bring herself to do that. "Steph, you must have been in some tricky situations back in the day, with Scott and Miranda and the others."

"Too many to mention."

"So what would you have done back then?"

"Luca, I don't know what stories you might or might not have heard about me, but I'm not the hero type. Your father was in command—well, kind of. He would usually come up with some outlandish plan, and your mother would kick anybody's ass who got in the way of that plan." She looked over at Luca with a wry smile. "They were a good team. Actually, we all were, especially Cyrus. He could always find a way to engineer us out of a tight spot." She paused for a moment. "If you ever get to the New World, you'll get to meet him. Tell him I said hello."

They sat there in silence for a while, watching the craft tread its way into the tangled, messy expanse of the orbital station.

"I can see how it would be easy to hide a small ship in this labyrinth," said Luca, after they passed the outer edges of some sprawling structure.

The Johnston Transit Orbital was not one big space station. It was a tangled mess of interconnected units, some seemingly attached by nothing more than a long, thin strut to carry wiring and pipes, while others looked to be completely detached. It was like an archipelago of islands in space. Some close enough to be connected by bridges, and some yet to be connected, all clustered around a group of four or five large sectors.

Luca glanced at the 3D navigation schematic on the central holo-screen, then back at the feed on the main monitor, and pointed at an isolated structure ahead. "There. That's where the ship is heading, that section over there."

"Are you sure? No lights. No other ships that I can see. Looks completely abandoned."

"Perfect drop-off location for a crew of smugglers."

Luca pointed again. "There's a long gantry extending out to it from that other sector."

"We should be able to get to the main transit area through that." Steph looked over at Luca. "Okay, we better get ready. Here's what I suggest we do. Grab some weapons, open that container with the crew, and Fly can shoot a few more of those darts into them."

"With pleasure," announced the drone.

"Good, that will put them out for a few more hours. Then, we take it real slow and quiet, and find our way to the main transit sector. That's where the ship with your ticket to New World One should be."

Luca thought about this for a moment. She would have preferred to take her chances getting to the Belt on this ship. But Steph had not intended to go any further than the orbital. So, Luca would be on her own from here.

"Unless you've got a better plan?" Steph was getting a little impatient with Luca's lack of response—they were only a few minutes from docking.

"Yeah, we have a better plan, alright," a new voice bellowed out from behind them.

Luca spun her head around to see the three crew floating into the flight deck, fully suited up and pointing plasma weapons. They must have woken up and somehow escaped from the shipping container.

"You pair of bozos. You don't think getting out of our own containers would be the first thing we learned?"

In the corner of her eye, Luca could see that Fly had

detached itself from the interface port and gathered itself up into a crouch, as if preparing to spring. She had no idea what it was planning, if anything. But its feeble weapons system was useless against the heavy EVA suits that the crew were now wearing, presumably for that very reason.

One of them noticed Fly and snapped his weapon up to fire at it.

"Whoa." Another of the crew grabbed the muzzle of the weapon and forced it back down. "Are you fucking crazy? You're gonna fry every circuit board in the flight deck."

Fly seized the moment and took off, scuttling across the ceiling, disappearing into a ventilation shaft.

"Shit, it got away."

"Doesn't matter, it can't do anything. Those darts can't penetrate the suits. Leave it, it's not important. Just tie them up. Good and tight this time."

16

MANUAL OVERRIDE

L uca and Steph were tied up and strapped into two crew seats on the flight deck while the ship went through its docking maneuvers. But so far, none of the crew had realized Luca still wore the neural lace. She reckoned that being off-grid types, they were not familiar with the technology and didn't realize that it was she who controlled the drone.

Yet there was not much she could do unless she activated the interface, and that required using her hands that were bound tight with her arms strapped down by the seat harness. But even if she could somehow manage to reach up to it, what could the drone do? Its weapons' system was useless against thick EVA suits. Maybe she could get it to disable the ship, but that would mean the drone exposing itself, as it needed to use the interface on the cockpit console.

She twisted her pinned arms a little and reckoned she

could get them free of the seat harness, but not while she was being watched. The best she could hope for was to wait for an opportunity, a time when they weren't being monitored, then try and figure out what she could get the drone to do, if anything.

There was a clunk followed by the sound of the locking bolts firing. When the ship was finally secured, the new captain swiveled around in his seat and looked at Luca.

"Seems these VanHeilding guys want you real bad. They've sent a few of their agents here to pick you up. So we're going to deliver you as promised, and then me and the guys are going to retire." He waved a hand around at the others. "No more of this bullshit ducking and diving."

He turned to one of the crew. "Becker, go check out the area outside. Make sure it's all nice and quiet." He gestured with a jerk of his head toward the airlock. Then he turned to the other crew member. "Dillon, go find that drone and destroy it. Can't be too many places it can hide on this ship."

The two crew closed their helmet visors and floated out of the flight deck. The new captain returned to studying the ship's flight console. Luca and Steph exchanged glances. With the captain distracted and the two crew occupied with their respective tasks, Luca tested the harness that secured her to the seat. Her efforts were hampered by her constant checking of the captain's focus. He would shift in his seat, halting her efforts, only to resume his study of the navigation screen.

She finally wriggled her hands free, reached up to the back of her head, and activated the neural lace. As her mind began to make the connection, she shoved her hands back under the harness and focused on the drone.

"Where are you?"

A ship schematic blossomed into view in her mind's eye, highlighting Fly's location, deep within the network of ventilation ducts.

"One of them is looking for you, Fly."

"Yes, I have sensed him moving around, shining lights into ducts and alcoves. His efforts are futile, he will not find me."

"VanHeilding agents are coming, we don't have much time. We need to do something."

"I fear my options are limited. I could try and cut you free, but I might not have sufficient time before I'm spotted. However, I could disable the ship and prevent it from operating."

"We're leaving the ship, so that's no use, unless you could disable the airlock door."

"That might be possible. But it would only buy a little time as there is a manual override that..."

Luca lost the connection, as her mind was snapped back to the here and now by the captain's sudden movement. He was talking into his comms unit. "Listen up, guys. The VanHeilding people are on their way, they'll be here in a few minutes. Let's get these ladies unpacked and brought outside. We can do the handover there."

Luca struggled to reconnect with the drone, but her

mind refused to disengage from the current threat. It was on hyper-alert and singularly focused on the moment.

The other two crew floated onto the flight deck at almost at the same time. The captain waved a hand at Luca and Steph. "Get them out of the seats. We'll take them outside. Come on, let's get this done."

They undid the seat harnesses and pulled them both out of their seats, and began to push them out of the flight deck.

It was difficult for Luca to get orientated in the zero-gee environment with her hands and feet tied. She did manage to catch a look from Steph. One that said, *If you're going to do something with that drone, now would be a good time.*

The airlock cycled through its normal opening procedure, meaning that Fly had failed to disable it. It was her last hope; now there would be nothing between Luca and the agents that had come for her.

17

AGENTS

The airlock opened onto a short docking tunnel. Luca and Steph were pushed out and nudged forward. The tunnel quickly transitioned into a broader corridor and finally out into a wide warehousing area. It was dimly lit, and grubby with age and disuse.

Two agents were there to meet them, clad in clean, sharp urban attire complete with mag-boots that enabled them to secure themselves to most metal surfaces. Their look was a far cry from the grubbiness of the smugglers' EVA suits. And judging by the augmented reality headsets and the sophisticated weapons clipped to their waistbands, these were not people to be messed with.

"Vance, I presume?" one of them called out.

"Yes, that's me." The captain floated forward. "We have what you came for." He jerked his head at Luca.

"Good. Bring her over, we'll take it from here."

"Whoa, buddy, hold on there a moment. There's a small matter of payment."

The two agents looked at one another for a brief moment, as if silently discussing this issue. Finally, the black-haired dude spoke. "Your contract was to bring her to the lunar rendezvous coordinates. Payment was dependent on this being executed. Since you failed in your mission, the contract is null and void."

The atmosphere in the warehouse suddenly changed, as if it was experiencing a sudden decompression.

Vance raised an arm in front of Luca and slowly turned to the other crew. "Let's move the merchandise back out of the way for a moment while we discuss this."

Luca felt herself being pushed way back down into the connecting tunnel along with Steph. She tumbled a little before grabbing some cables that were floating out from the side wall. As she did, she managed to snag Steph with her feet. The doctor pulled herself along Luca's legs and grabbed onto the cables.

"Stay there, and don't even think of moving." One of the crew had followed them back and took up a position off to one side, a little forward of them.

Ahead, Luca could see a lot of hand-waving and macho posturing by both groups. She couldn't hear much, but she didn't need to make out the words being exchanged to figure out that neither side was giving ground. It could be an opportunity, if only there wasn't a crew member right in front of them.

"Where's that drone?" Steph whispered. "Things

could get messy here and give us an opportunity, maybe to sneak back onto the ship."

The prospect of escape, even if remote, made Luca's brain kick back into gear, and she felt the presence of the drone again.

As she suspected, it could not get the airlock disabled in time, but was now outside the ship clinging to the side of the access tunnel, just a few meters from where they clung to the cables.

"My apologies for not being able to assist you so far. But my ability to move fast in this environment is poor."

"Just hang back for a moment."

Luca shifted her position so she could whisper to Steph without being noticed. "It's here, in the tunnel, very close to us."

The doctor took a moment to look around her, examining the access tunnel structure. "Okay, I have an idea," she whispered in reply. "This guy is not holding onto anything, just floating there. So I'm going to kick him as hard as I can. The instant I do, you let go of that cable. He'll go tumbling forward and we'll go backward down the tunnel. Get that drone ready to jump on us and cut these bonds. Got it?"

Luca let the drone know the plan and then nodded to Steph.

She reacted almost instantly, bringing her knees up to her chest and kicking out hard with both feet, slamming them into the smuggler's back. Luca released her grip, and they went tumbling back down the access tunnel.

Luca lost all orientation as the tunnel spun around her. She heard shouts, then the *whomp, whomp* of a plasma weapon. "Shit, they're shooting at us. Fly, where the hell are you?"

She felt something grab onto her back, then scuttle around to her bound hands and cut the ties. She reached out, trying to find something to grab to stop the tumbling. A grab handle spun by her field of vision; she reached out and got a grip on it. Her body twisted back against the side wall of the access tunnel just as a plasma blast shot past her, dissipating harmlessly far off down at the other end of the tunnel.

Her feet were now free and so was Steph, who still clung on to Luca's flight suit. Fly was back on the side wall, watching and waiting.

"Let's get to the ship." Steph pointed back up the tunnel to the docking port and started moving. Luca followed. Up ahead, she could see a firefight had broken out between the two groups. So they were not trying to shoot her or Steph, they were shooting at each other. A body floated down the tunnel behind them, its EVA suit burned and scorched on the chest.

Steph grabbed Luca's arm and pulled her into the ship's airlock; Fly scuttled in after them. They slammed the door shut and spun the locking mechanism.

"We have to get this ship the hell out of here. You think you can fly it?" Steph hit the button to open the inner door.

"Yeah, I think so."

They hurried to the flight deck and strapped themselves in. Fly connected to the interface, and Luca's mind was instantly assailed by ship data. Somewhere outside she thought she heard banging on the airlock door.

"Hurry," said Steph. "They're trying to get in."

Luca's mind raced, her synapses firing at quantum speed as she delved into the ship's systems, but something was different this time. Where before she had been overcome by fear, anxiety brought on by the overwhelming scale of the data coming at her, now she rode it like a surfer catching a wave. She found the docking systems, found that the ship had been put into lockdown by the orbiting station, and simply disabled it as if it were nothing. She felt the thump as it detached. The vernier thrusters fired, pushing the ship out into free space. By now, another part of her mind had initiated the navigation system to chart a course. She paused, brought herself out of the mind-machine interface for a brief second, and turned to Steph.

"Better get ready, we're going to the New World."

Steph simply nodded and tightened her seat harness.

Luca reentered the ship's systems and gave the command to initiate the primary drive. Instantly, they were slammed deep into their seats as the ship accelerated away from the Johnston Transit Orbital and out into interplanetary space.

18

CRAZY TIMES

M iranda would not reach New World One for many weeks, so Scott had desperately wanted to borrow a fast ship from Cyrus and head back to Earth and search for Luca. But in reality, what would that achieve? Both Miranda and Cyrus already had their own networks of people scouring the Johnston Transit Orbital for any sign of Luca or Steph. Not only that, but the QIs had assured him that if the pair were anywhere on that orbital, or even back on Earth, then they would find them. So what use would Scott be? In the end, it was Miranda who had finally persuaded him to stay put on New World One and wait for her. Part of him was a little flattered; maybe she just wanted to see him again. And if he was being true to himself, he had to admit that he really wanted to see her again, too—after all these years. In the end, he resisted the desire to journey to Earth and instead got on with what Cyrus regarded as the most important job on the habitat—getting the defense system up and running.

So here he was, encased in an EVA suit, attached by a tether to the exterior hull of New World One, overseeing the installation of a plasma cannon battery. It had been part of Cyrus's contract, and with the increasing paranoia permeating the Belt, he was understandably anxious to get it operational. He had been working on it for weeks; at least it kept his mind off things.

It didn't help that rumors were spreading of a well-armed ghost ship spotted on the far side of Luna and now heading for the Belt. But what troubled Scott more was that the QIs were being very circumspect about these rumors, meaning that they simply didn't know. This led him and many others to believe that the army of Node Runners utilized by the Seven had become far more adept at cloaking their activities within the Grid. All that could be relied on now was visual observation. And in the vast expanse of space, it would be impossible to find even the largest ship by simply eyeballing it.

SCOTT WAS KEEPING a close eye on his readouts as the first of two plasma gun turrets was being floated into position. The second one would be mounted on the opposite side of the cylinder. But even when that was completed, there would still be at least another few weeks of work in connecting all the power and control systems before testing could begin. He was feeling the pressure. They all were.

His comms burst into life. "Scott, Cyrus here. I think I got something. You'd better hand over to someone there and meet me in the ops room as soon as you can."

"You mean you got something on Luca and Steph?"

"Yeah, one of my guys came good and turned up something on Johnston. You need to take a look."

"You know where they are?"

"No, but I think I know where they might be. Just get your ass down here."

"Are they okay?"

"Scott, it's best if I show you rather than over comms."

"Okay, on my way."

IT TOOK him the best part of an hour to hand over to his crew buddy, get back inside the habitat, take off his bulky EVA suit, then travel the three kilometers to the location of the ops room that Cyrus and the other main contractors used for planning and monitoring the complex construction process of New World One.

Like all structures in the habitat, it was a sprawling open-plan space populated with numerous people gathered around holo-tables and monitors. Scott looked around for Cyrus and eventually found him in a glass-walled side meeting room. He signaled to Scott to come in and join him.

"Scott, great, you're here. Check this out."

Scott moved over beside Cyrus and looked down at the video feed streaming on the table screen. "What am I looking at here?"

"This is a feed from an external source on the Johnston Transit Orbital, around four weeks ago."

Scott studied the feed. As far as he could tell from the grainy images, it was focused on a derelict sector of the vast orbital—no lights, no activity, totally devoid of life. "I don't see anything going on here."

"Perfect place for a smuggler to dock, don't you think?"

Scott glanced up at Cyrus with raised eyebrows. "You mean…"

Cyrus cut him off with a wave at the screen. "Look at this." He tapped a few icons, the image zoomed in, and Scott could now see a blurry image of a small ship docked to the derelict sector.

"That's Weismann's ship. The guy who was supposed to take Luca and Steph off Earth."

"Holy shit, Cyrus. You found them. This is great. Are they okay?"

Cyrus stood up and turned to face Scott. "Let me back up a bit and give you the full story. I had some contacts of mine do some investigating on Captain Weismann. He's a good guy, someone I trust, so the question is what happened to the mission. Anyway, we started by checking out old sectors in the orbital we knew he used in the past." Cyrus pointed at the screen. "When he checked out this sector, he discovered three bodies. And no, none are Luca or Steph. Just three unknowns. Then we did some background checks, and it turns out all three of them had been on Weismann's crew at various times in the past."

Scott looked down at the screen again. "What happened? And where's Luca?"

"There was a firefight of some kind. All three died from plasma blasts, and the bodies hastily hidden. It was just a bit of luck that my man found them. But whatever happened didn't last very long, as the ship departed almost as soon as it arrived."

"You think Luca and Steph are still on it?"

"Looks that way."

"This is great work, Cyrus. So where are they now?"

Cyrus gave a wry smile. "Ah, good question." It was clear the engineer was relishing this exposé. "I recruited the help of Aria to do some analysis now that we had some data on the ship. You have to remember that this ship is off-grid, so the QIs had nothing to work with. But Aria analyzed all visual data-feeds in and around the Johnston Transit Orbital during that period." He turned back to the screen. "Have a look at this."

A new feed showed mostly space with just a small section of the orbital visible in the bottom left corner. As it played, Scott could see the same ship come into view, power up its main engines, and disappear into the void. "Where are they going?"

"Aria has given a high probability that the ship is heading for deep space. And given that Mars is currently on the other side of the sun, there's nothing else out there until they hit the Belt."

"The Belt? But that's an old orbit hopper. There's no way that can do interplanetary travel."

"It might look like a bucket of bolts, but it has a VASMIR main engine, so it's well capable of entering deep space."

Scott stood up, scratched his chin, and started to pace around. "So they're heading to us." He stopped suddenly. "Any comms? Have you tried contacting the ship?"

"Nada. Both Aria and Homer checked all the comms activity for that region. Nothing. But we wouldn't expect anything until it comes into range of a relay beacon."

"They could be in trouble, Cyrus. I need to head out there and find them, and find them now."

"Whoa, hold up. You would never find a ship that small out there unless you crash into it."

"I know, but I gotta try, Cyrus. I can't sit here and do nothing now that we have an idea where they are. Have you sent this to Miranda?"

"Yeah, just after I called you. No word back yet. She's still another three days away."

Scott stayed silent for a moment, thinking.

"Listen, Scott, there's no point in you heading out into the void, not unless you have a reasonable set of coordinates for their location." Cyrus moved over to a holo-table and tapped a few icons to bring up a 3D schematic of the local sector of Belt space. "There are at least three relay beacons covering most of the approach vectors from Earth's position when they departed. But just bear in mind that even if the ship passes one, that doesn't mean we'll pick it up."

"How so?"

"Remember, it's off-grid. So unless they want to relay messages and make a connection to the beacon, we won't know if they're there."

"Hmmm...and if they are trying to keep hidden, then they're probably not going to expose themselves."

"Exactly. Who knows what else is out there?"

"You're not still going on about that ghost ship, are you?"

"I don't know, Scott. Aria is pretty spooked. Homer, too. I've never seen the QIs that uncertain about anything in my life. As you can imagine, it's a little disconcerting."

"You think this so-called ghost ship might be chasing them down?"

"Anything is possible, Scott. It could be heading our way, there could be more than one, who knows. But what I do know is it's not good. Something major is about to happen. That what's got the QIs so cagey. They sense something is going on, but not what it is or where it's going to go down."

Scott shook his head. "Crazy times, Cyrus. I feel as if nothing makes sense anymore. The old certainties are gone now that we can't rely on the QI network to keep a lid on things." Scott glanced back at the schematic and pointed to one of the beacon markers. "How long would it take to get to any of these beacons here?"

Cyrus leaned in. "Three days, maybe less if you were prepared to black out under heavy acceleration."

"And how soon do you think Weismann's ship will come into range?"

"Hard to say, but it should be soon. They may be already be in range."

Scott nodded. "Now what? Do I head out there, or wait for them to get here and try o send a message?"

"Maybe do both. Get ready to go, I'll get you a fast ship. Then wait a day or two to see if there's any contact. If not, then head out. But remember, you're unlikely to find them by just wandering around out there."

Scott gave out a long sigh. "Yeah, I know that. But put yourself in my shoes. If there is even the smallest chance of finding them, then I have to take it."

19

THIRST

A part from the initial ten-hour acceleration burn, the first few days of the journey from the Johnston Transit Orbital had been relatively easy, and both Luca and Dr. Rayman began to relax a little.

But soon their attentions turned to the issue of food and water, and how to make the meager provisions last the next forty-four days they estimated it would take to reach New World One. Steph spent some time analyzing the nutrients available and rationed out the food as best she could. She presented Luca with a minuscule portion, explaining to her that this was it for the next twenty-four hours, then went to great lengths to reassure her that it was possible to live for thirty or so days without food. This did not comfort Luca in any way; it simply underscored her own acceptance that it was going to be a very long and hungry trip.

Although the average healthy human could theoretically live for weeks without food, water was a different matter entirely. They kept the environment and the ship cool so that they would not be wasting water through perspiration, even though the ship had a reasonably efficient recycling system. But based on the reserves they had on board, it became obvious that they would be slowly dehydrating as the days passed. Even the best recycling system could not produce more water than it collected.

By day seven, they were both finding it difficult to focus on anything other than food—it was all Luca thought about, and almost the only thing she and Steph talked about. They spent many days sharing stories of memorable meals and culinary delights. But by day fourteen, all this had passed as they both settled into survival mode, barely moving or even speaking, expending minimal energy.

ON DAY THIRTY-EIGHT, the water finally ran out. Luca was strapped into the pilot seat on the flight deck when Steph floated in and handed her a small metal flask.

"Here you go, this is the last I could wring out of the recycler. It's only a few milliliters."

Luca twisted off the cap and took a sip. The water was brackish with a stale taste. Nonetheless, it felt like nectar from the gods as it made its way down her parched throat. "A few sips are not going to last us six more days."

Steph shrugged. She was a doctor, after all—she knew the score. They sat there quietly for a time, each deep in their own thoughts.

Luca's attention eventually returned to the 3D navigational schematic of their current position that blossomed out of the central holo-screen. In one quadrant, a small section of the asteroid belt was depicted with a marker at one end, indicating the location of the dwarf planet, Ceres. Another marker at the far end indicated the location of New World One— their ultimate destination. They were almost there. It was only six long, hard days away.

The projection flickered a little as Steph suddenly poked her finger at a marker, seemingly positioned in the middle of nowhere. "What's that?"

Luca glanced at the projection. "I don't know. There's a few of them. See, here's another one." She tapped the projection to highlight it.

"Those look like relay beacons to me," said Steph. "And that one is almost directly in our travel path." She tapped the marker, and immediately a cascade of data spewed out on a side monitor.

"What's a relay beacon?" Luca leaned over and tried reading the data on screen.

"Think of it as a Grid Node, except in space. They're used for routing data and communications as well as navigation."

"Are you saying it can broadcast our location?"

"I don't think so, not unless we connect with it. But to

be honest, Luca, I'm not sure about that. What I do know is that these beacons are technically very complex and need regular maintenance. They're autonomous, but all have accommodation for maintenance crew visits. However, the most interesting thing is they are generally very well provisioned." She looked over at Luca. "That means food and water."

At the mention of this, Luca perked up. "Food and water?"

"Yep." Steph reached down to the holo-screen and adjusted the navigation map, zooming in on the relay beacon. "I'm just guessing here, but it looks to be around a day away."

Luca studied the marker on the 3D navigation schematic with all the intensity of a hungry wolf.

"If we wanted to go there, then you would have to do that thing you do... You know, with the drone."

Luca glanced over at Steph. "I reckon I could do that. I think I just have to set the navigation parameters for that location, and the ship's systems will plot a course and calculate the burn we'll need to slow down—which is going to be pretty hardcore. If we did ten hours leaving the Transit Orbital, we'll need at least the same." Luca looked at the marker again. "The only thing is, if we were to dock at that beacon, would we pop up on the Grid?"

Steph thought about this for a moment. "I really don't know, but I guess we'd show up somewhere, even if it's just on some log for whomever's in charge of maintaining that facility."

"Which means," said Luca, "that anybody looking for us would know exactly where we are."

"I know, it's a risk. But even though we're only six days away from New World One, that's a very long time with just a few milliliters of water between us. We may not survive, and even if we do, we may not be in a fit state to deal with any eventualities that might crop up. So yeah, it's a risk. But knowing where we are and getting to us are two different things entirely, and that facility is most likely in the domain of the QI, Homer, on Ceres." Steph raised a finger just to emphasize the point.

"Screw it, we'll go. I'm too malnourished and dehydrated to care anymore." Luca tapped the back of her skull to activate the neural net and get the show on the road.

"Yeah, me too," said Steph with a sigh.

20

BEACON 23

Luca had become quite adept at interfacing with the ship's systems during the many weeks they had been on board. She had little else to do, and it kept her mind off the hunger. So it took her no time to connect via the drone and set the necessary navigation parameters for the relay beacon. The ship slowly began to rotate itself 180 degrees so that the engines now faced the direction of travel. This maneuver gave Luca and Steph just enough time to strap themselves down tight. When the retro-burn finally kicked in, Luca was slammed back into her seat, pinned there with the extreme force of the acceleration. They were pulling a lot of gees and would be unable to move for the next ten or so hours.

SOMETIME DURING THE BURN, Luca blacked out and only

came to when Steph jabbed her with a shot of something from the meager medical kit she carried.

"Here, drink this." Steph held the flask with the last of the water to Luca's lips. "Drink it all, there's only a few drops anyway."

The fuzziness in her brain started to clear and Luca began to take stock of her surroundings. "Are we there? Did we make it?"

"Yeah, we made it—see." Steph moved back to her seat and Luca could now see the silhouette of the relay beacon looming large through the flight deck window. Any thoughts she had of staying off-grid and keeping a low profile vanished; all she could think about now was food and water.

She stared fixedly at the navigation beacon, watching it grow in size as the ship slowly approached. She felt like a weary traveler lost in the desert, now crawling her way inch by inch to a lonely, isolated diner by the edge of a dusty road.

As they moved alongside the docking port, the cockpit navigation console suddenly came to life. The ship now began to negotiate the final procedure with the beacon. Luca glanced over at Steph. "I presume this is the moment that we pop up on the Grid?"

Steph looked at the data scrolling down the screen. "I guess so. We'd better be quick."

SUCH WAS their impatience to find food and water that

they were already floating beside the airlock, listening for every sound, even before the docking sequence had finished. As soon as the side panel illuminated green, Luca punched the button to enter.

The outer door opened directly into a comparatively large circular living space designed for a maintenance crew to lay over for a few days. It didn't take them long to find the galley and start cracking open a storage container that was clearly marked with a large water droplet and the words *drinking water* in several languages. Luca pulled out two pouches, lobbed one over to Steph, broke the seal on the other, and started to drink. As the cool, clear liquid began soothing her parched throat, she reckoned that it was the most delicious thing she had ever tasted in her life.

"Go easy with that, Luca," Steph said as she broke the seal on the water pouch. "Don't drink too much or you'll end up throwing it up. Just take a few sips at a time."

Luca's next target was a pouch of freeze-dried noodles. She broke the tab to activate the inbuilt hydrator and chemical heater. But she couldn't wait the two minutes it took to finish processing, and instead broke it open and started shoving the dry, brittle noodles into her mouth. Nevertheless, it was the second most amazing thing she had ever tasted.

They spent the next half hour eating and drinking, barely saying a word other than expressing just how delicious everything tasted.

Steph wiped her mouth with the back of her hand. "I

suppose we'd better get going. It wouldn't do to stay here too long."

"Yeah, we can grab some supplies and bring them back to the ship. We're not going to need that much, it's only another five days to get there."

"I was thinking..." Steph began gathering up a couple of food containers. "Now that we've probably popped up on the Grid, maybe we should just send a message to Cyrus on New World One, let him know we're alive and well and heading that way."

"You think that would be safe?"

"If we wanted to be safe, then we wouldn't be doing this." She waved a hand around. "My guess is they know where we are now, so sending a message to Cyrus isn't going to make any difference."

THEY HEADED BACK to the ship. Steph stowed the provisions while Luca strapped herself into the pilot seat, activated her neural lace, and connected to the ship's systems. But as she entered the data-stream, she sensed a disturbance—something was not quite right. Luca sought out the docking subsystem and instructed it to undock the ship—but nothing happened.

What the heck? Her first reaction was that she was not concentrating properly; she was still very weak from the journey. She tried again—still nothing. She probed the drone for its analysis.

"Any idea what's going on with the ship systems, Fly? I can't undock from the beacon."

"I suspect we're being hacked."

"Hacked?" A momentary surge of panic rose up in Luca. "How can that be possible? Who's doing this?"

"The ship is connected to the Grid via the relay beacon. So theoretically, anyone with sufficient knowledge and skill could gain access."

"But we're within the domain of the QI on Ceres." Yet even as Luca said these words, she realized she could not sense its presence.

"The QI was destroyed in an attack on Ceres approximately two hours ago, according to the newsfeeds I am accessing."

Luca suddenly lost the neural connection, such was her shock. Steph, now strapped into her seat, could sense something was wrong. "What is it, Luca? You look like you've seen a ghost."

Luca's head slowly rotated and faced the doctor, her mouth open, her eyes wide. "The QI, Homer...it's been...destroyed."

Steph's face morphed into a look of incredulity. "Are you sure? How do you know?"

Luca tried to concentrate and reconnect with the ship, but she was not in the right frame of mind. "Fly?" she said out loud. "Can you display one of those newsfeeds on the main monitor?"

"Holy crap." The doctor's reaction was instant. On screen, an aerial view of Rongo City on Ceres showed what remained of one of the city's research habitats, the one housing the QI, Homer.

"Oh my God, they actually did it. They took out a QI." Steph looked over at Luca. "We'd better get going, we can't hang around here any longer."

"I can't—the ship won't undock. I tried, but it just won't disengage. Fly thinks we've been hacked."

"This is bad, Luca. Real bad. They must know we're here...and are preventing us from leaving." She then looked directly at Luca. "That means they're coming for us...for you. You've got to get us out of here."

Luca shook her head. "I've tried, but it just won't respond."

Steph remained silent for a moment, then leaned over and spoke in a low, calm tone. "Listen, Luca, you need to understand what they will do to you if they find us still here. You have to try and get the ship free of this facility. You need to do whatever it takes."

Luca lowered her head and gave a slight nod. "Okay, I'll try."

21

THE DATA-STREAM

L uca slowly regained her composure, reached up to the back of her head, and activated the neural lace. Immediately, she could feel the tendrils moving across her skull, seeking out connections. Her mind now focused on Fly. "Can I still get a message to New World One?" she asked.

"No, I'm afraid not. All communication must be relayed through the beacon, and the data paths are inoperable."

Yet Luca already knew that this would be the answer, so she moved past Fly and into the ship's own data-stream. She had become very familiar with it, having spent so much time interfacing with the systems over the last couple of weeks. So much so, that she could tell what was native data and what was alien. She sifted through the data, focusing on the foreign invasion. In her mind's eye, she could see it as fuzzy, crude tendrils, in complete contrast to the elegant filaments of native data. It had to be coming in through the ship's interface with the beacon. Luca paused for a beat as she steeled herself for the inevitable onslaught of data that awaited her on the far side of that interface. When she was ready, she dived in and followed it.

Her mind exploded with a billion particles of data. They fizzed and danced as the beacon relayed communications to and from its network of sister beacons scattered throughout the solar system. Luca was mesmerized by it. She had assumed that entering the beacon's data-stream would be too much for her, overload her mind like her first encounter with the ship's own systems. But this was a vision of harmony and order. This was beauty, this was poetry.

Yet to undock the ship she needed to follow the trail, taking her deeper into the network, beyond the beacon. As she got closer to its source, she began to sense a presence, another human in the data-stream. She recoiled slightly. The thought of someone else in the system, or possibly more, meant only one thing—Node Runners, probably the very same people who attacked the Grid Node on Earth and the QI on Ceres.

But they sensed her, too, and a mass of new tendrils suddenly snaked out of the data-stream, seeking her out. Luca retreated; they followed. She retreated further, recoiling against the probing filaments that were hunting her down. She had no choice but to disconnect from the system.

Her breathing was labored, her heart rate was elevated, and she was sweating profusely.

Steph leaned over and gave her that look all doctors give when they're very concerned. "Luca, are you okay?" She put a hand on her shoulder.

"They're in there, in the system. Trying to find me."

"Who? Who's in there, Luca?"

"Ghosts, Node Runners. Lots of them."

"Just take a few deep breaths, calm yourself down."

Luca followed the doctor's advice, the panic resided, and she could feel her heart rate dropping. "I'm okay." Luca waved a hand at Steph. "Just give me a minute to get myself together."

Steph handed her a pouch of water. "Here, drink some. You need to rehydrate."

Luca felt better with each sip. "I need to go back in. We have to get out of here."

"Are you sure you're up to it?"

Luca cocked her head to one side. "Do I have a choice?"

Steph screwed her face up a little. "Be careful."

Luca gave her a smile. "Don't worry, I'll try not to fry my brain."

She tapped the neural lace again and reentered the data-stream. But this time she hung back, simply observing, trying to get a bird's-eye view and building a picture of what the Node Runners were doing. She saw their tendrils snaking out in all directions into the ship's subsystems. Luca followed them, hanging back, not going as deep as she had before. She was like a hunter hiding in the tall grass, observing her prey, waiting for her moment.

They had disabled the docking mechanism, rendering it inoperable—this was why the ship could not leave. But Luca also sensed them actively seeking out other systems, probing the engine drive, life-support, and power. They were trying to do more than just prevent the ship from leaving. Yet she could now see that all these attacks originated via the comms network. If she could block that, then maybe she could regain control of the ship long enough to disengage it from the beacon. And once disengaged, the Node Runners could not get back in again. She circled around the comms port, approaching it from different network nodes, building an understanding of its operational parameters.

But they spotted her, sensed what she was trying to do, and now focused their attention toward her. Yet this time, rather than retreating, Luca met them head-on. They were not expecting her to fight back, and she could sense their trepidation, perhaps even a little fear.

She pressed her advantage, pushing at them. They were slow to respond, but when they did, it was with greater intensity. Yet Luca repelled their efforts. As they opened up new data gateways, Luca closed them. When they tried to reroute their attacks, she blocked them. One by one, she closed down the avenues by which they could enter and gain access to the ship's system.

By the time she closed in on the primary comms port,

she could sense that a great many more Node Runners were being brought to bear on the task of fighting her off. Luca was finding it more difficult to push them back. She made one final effort and focused all her mental energy on getting control of the comms port and closing it.

Something snapped, and the Node Runners' attack suddenly collapsed. Luca felt herself tumbling through the comms port, carried by the momentum of her focus. Her mind sped past the cacophonous data-stream of the beacon, out through its comms link, and straight into the mind of the very last Node Runner who was trying to fight her off.

She halted, not sure what she was doing here—in the mind of another human. Yet it fascinated her, drew her in, and so she began to explore it—more from a benign curiosity than for any other reason. She probed deeper, seeking out some understanding of this Node Runner. It was clumsily trying to hide, to obscure its knowledge and memory from her inquiry. Luca swept aside its flimsy defenses, and then she saw it—a vision of a vast cargo hold, filled with row upon row of weaponized attack droids, all waiting to be unleashed.

Luca pulled back in horror, trying to digest what she had just seen. Was it real, or was it just some figment of the Node Runner's imagination? She couldn't be sure.

As Luca began to extricate her mind from the swirling sea of intersystem data, she paused momentarily within the beacon's network long enough to disentangle the spaceship from its mechanical grip. Part of her sensed it separate and drift free, although she could not be precisely sure if this had happened already, was currently happening, or had yet to happen. Nevertheless, she was certain that she had instigated the ship's release—she was sure of it.

Yet this strange time dilation that she was now experiencing intrigued her, so her mind began to explore it. Tentatively at first, probing the outer edges until she realized it was her own mind she was exploring and not some data-stack or system AI.

But it was not the crude stuff of memories, or the cumbersome verbiage of thoughts, nor was it some glacially slow philosophical pondering. No, this was brilliance and clarity—an enlightenment of sorts. She found it both exhilarating and eternal, like she had finally arrived at a place that was her destiny. It enveloped her, wrapped her up in a warm dreamlike blanket, and for the first time in her life, she felt she a deep, satisfying contentment. She belonged.

22

GHOST IN THE GRID

For a long time, there was nothing but stunned silence in the Sanato Corp. operations center on New World One as Scott, Cyrus, and some of his people all tried to come to terms with what had just happened on Ceres. Miranda also joined them from the Perception via a video link. She was still a few days away from arriving, but was already being pressed by the governing body of New World for her help in bolstering the habitat's defenses, as the new plasma cannons were not yet operational.

Many had been expecting something after the attack on the Grid Node on Earth. Yet the complete destruction of the QI, Homer on Ceres was beyond most people's ability to comprehend. They all knew they were witnessing a paradigm shift in the order of things. With the QI gone, this entire region of the Belt was vulnerable, including New World One.

"Any word from Solomon?" Scott said as he paced up and down along the viewing window that ran the length of the room, stopping every now and again to check the new alerts that popped up on the main monitor.

"Europa is quite a distance from us at the moment," Cyrus said as he too monitored the alerts coming in. "It will take time for a message to get here."

"Do they know if this was some homegrown terrestrial sabotage, or did it come from orbit?" Scott stopped his pacing. "I mean, do they know if there is a ship out there?"

One of Cyrus's people, a tech by the name of Jinty, jerked a finger at some data on her screen. "They're saying it looks like it's a direct missile strike from orbit... which would suggest it came from a ship. Reports are still sketchy," she continued. "Some are suggesting that a big freighter simply popped up out of nowhere. But that might be just a glitch."

"I don't believe this." Cyrus gestured in frustration. "Ceres attacked, Homer destroyed, and nobody seems to have a goddamn clue how it happened or who's behind this."

"We all know who's behind this." Miranda now joined the discussion. "Same as the destruction of the Grid Node back on Earth. This is clearly the work of the Seven and that megalomaniac Fredrick VanHeilding with his Node Runners. If he has a ship out there with a bunch of those weirdos on board, then it's no wonder people can't find it. The only way you can see that ship is if you crash into it."

"Optical." Cyrus raised a finger in the air as if some genius idea had just popped into his head.

"Optical? What the heck you talking about?" said Scott.

"An optical telescope. It's not on the Grid, not digital, it doesn't need to be connected to the data-stream, it just uses light waves. They can't hide from that."

"Seriously, Cyrus. Does anybody use optical telescopes anymore? That technology hasn't been around for centuries. Nobody uses them. And even if you did have one, you would need to know the precise point in space to look at."

"This is all irrelevant," Miranda snapped as she leaned into the camera, making her face almost fill the screen. "You need to get it into your heads that this is a tactical strike to make this entire area of space defenseless." She waved a hand around for emphasis. "Anything connected to the Grid is now at the mercy of those...Node Runners. That includes New World One. My guess is that's exactly where they're heading next— that's the prize, that's what they want. With the New World, VanHeilding and the other six families effectively have total control over the resources of the Belt."

"How long before those plasma cannon are operational?" Scott looked over at Cyrus. The engineer was sitting down, his head lowered, with the fingertips of one hand pressed up against his temple. Scott knew what this meant—Cyrus was accessing some data or communicating with someone using his neural interface. Yet Scott knew from the look on his face that he was struggling to comprehend something.

He was about to ask if everything was okay when Cyrus stood up and looked from Scott to Miranda and back again. "I just got something in, something a bit... well, weird. It's Luca."

He tapped on the side of his visor, then swept his hand out to send the data onto the main monitor.

A series of strange images cascaded across the screen. Scott found it hard to decipher what he was seeing. It looked like a factory floor, or a warehouse, or maybe even the cargo hold of some large freighter. Wherever it was, it was packed tight with row upon row of military robots—hundreds of them.

"Holy crap." Cyrus began fiddling with some controls to squeeze more definition from the images. "That looks like a goddamn droid army."

"What's this got to do with Luca?" Miranda's face was now so close to the camera that her image on screen was almost a blur.

"It's...hard to explain." Cyrus shook his head a little. "This data came from Luca on Weismann's orbit hopper. It's docked at Beacon 23, at the border of Belt space. But..." He looked confused. "The weird thing is it just suddenly arrived on the data-stack, like as if..." And here he paused for a moment, unsure of what to say. "As if she was in the system, in the data-stream, like a Node Runner."

"Luca? Are you sure?" Scott thought his old buddy was losing it.

"Is the ship still at the beacon?" Miranda had moved back a little from the camera and looked to be studying the images on the feed at her end.

"I don't know," said Cyrus. "Possibly. This just arrived a few moments ago."

"Beacon 23, that's around three days away from here." Jinty brought up a 3D schematic of that region of space on the main holo-table.

"I'm going to alter course and head for that beacon," said Miranda. "The Perception could get there in five days."

Scott thought for a moment. "Wait, Miranda. Let's think this through. Maybe it's better if I go. It would be quicker from here. Cyrus, do you have a ship I can borrow?"

"Sure do. I've got a very fast rock hopper. It should get you there in two days."

"Then that's it," said Scott. "I'll head for that relay beacon and try to locate Weismann's ship."

Miranda looked frustrated. Scott could tell she was itching to do something, but she was still too far away. "Okay." She nodded. "But please find her, Scott."

"I will, you better believe it." He turned back to Cyrus. "You'd better get those cannons operational as fast as humanly possible. If New World One is the target, then we've only got a few days before that ghost ship gets here from Ceres."

"Jeez, don't I know."

"Scott." Miranda leaned into the camera. "If you find Luca and Steph, maybe it's not a good idea to bring them back to the New World. It could be a shitstorm there."

"First thing's first, Miranda. I need to find them, then we can figure out what to do."

23

SECOND SHIP

Cyrus wasn't joking when he said the rock hopper was fast. Scott nearly passed out immediately after he punched the coordinates for Beacon 23 into the navigation system and hit initiate. What followed were three hours of the most intense acceleration he had ever experienced. Next time, he would dial back on the settings; perhaps maximum thrust was a bit extreme.

He came out of the burn period to a number of messages from Cyrus on the comms. They were using encrypted X Band. It was old-school, but it was off-grid so not as susceptible to being intercepted.

The New World people were working hard to take the habitat off the Grid and shut down all possible routes into its systems. But that was not as simple as it sounded. Most of the technology relied on connections to external data sources, and disconnection generally meant that they ceased to function. No one had ever considered this when they were designing the systems. No one in their right mind could have imagined any reason that a facility might need to operate independent of the data-stream.

But the meat of Cyrus's message was to let him know that the VanHeilding ship had now popped up on the Grid—it was no longer trying to hide itself. Presumably, since the QI had been eliminated, they now felt safe enough to expose themselves. But the good news, if you could call it that, was the ship hadn't moved from its position in Ceres orbit. So maybe New World One wasn't a target—yet.

They had also identified the ship as being one of two VanHeilding ships spotted loitering on the far side of Luna many weeks ago. Meaning that there might be a second VanHeilding ship out there somewhere. The bottom line was that Scott should be careful, as he may have company.

BY THE TIME he came out of the final retro-burn to slow the ship down, it had been a little over twenty hours since his departure from the New World. Outside, through the ship's forward window, he could see the relay beacon dead ahead. He was still some way out, so he brought up a view on the main monitor and zoomed in—then he saw it. A beat-up old orbit hopper floating in space around a kilometer from the main structure. *Damn,* he thought. *Dead in the water. Not good.*

He tried hailing it, but there was no answer. So over the next few hours, he guided his ship up close and did a quick visual pass of the craft. There was no damage that he could see other than the odd scorch mark here and there that may or may not have been the result of a plasma blast. But it all looked superficial and historic. Simply scars from its life as a smugglers' ship. There was nothing to indicate that it had suffered any recent physical damage.

Scott set his own ship to maintain a close stationary position relative to the dead orbit hopper, unfastened his seat harness, and made his way to the airlock, where he donned a heavy-duty miner's EVA suit that he'd found in one of the side lockers. He clipped on the helmet and checked the suit had enough resources. Finally, he stowed a compact plasma pistol he had brought with him into a cargo pocket, stepped into the airlock, and hit the button for decompression.

Before the outer door opened, he attached himself to a spooling tether to make sure he wouldn't get separated from the ship. Even if he got disoriented, he would be able to pull himself back to safety.

The outer door slid open and Scott found himself looking directly at the roof of the orbit hopper. He pushed himself out of the airlock, crossing the distance between the two ships in a few seconds. He aimed for a cluster of hand holds on one side of the secondary airlock, but he was moving faster than he had planned and hit the outer hull hard, yet managed to grab on before he bounced off again. "Sloppy," he said to himself. Anyone inside the ship would have heard the thump when he hit.

Scott took a second to gather himself and then moved, hand over hand, to the manual airlock mechanism. As he turned it, the outer door began to crack open, inch by inch. After a few moments, it was wide enough for him to crawl through. He unclipped the tether, attaching it to one of the exterior handholds, then proceeded to wind the door closed from the inside.

When it finally shut and repressurized, he pressed the button to open the inner door, and was immediately hit by a plasma blast, square on the chest. He slammed back into the outer airlock door, bounced off, and started tumbling about, completely losing his orientation. Fortunately, the tough EVA suit took the blast and he was uninjured. But it took him a second or two to orient himself, extract his plasma pistol, and seek out the assailant. Who turned out to be none other than Dr. Stephanie Rayman, wearing a look of complete shock on her face, probably equal to his own.

He put away his weapon and flipped open his visor. "Steph, glad to see you're still alive."

"Scott? Oh god, I'm sorry. I didn't know who the hell was scraping around out there on the hull trying to get in. Are you okay?"

"Fine. Fortunately, I'm wearing a miner's suit." He tapped the chest plate. "Tougher than an asteroid."

Steph reached a hand out and grabbed his arm. "I

can't believe it's you. I don't know how you found us, Scott. But I'm very glad you did, I thought I was going to die out here."

They floated out of the airlock. "Where's Luca?"

A concerned look came over Steph's face. "She's here. She's okay, but..."

"What? What's wrong?"

Steph jerked her head. "Come, I'll bring you to her."

They moved across the cargo hold to a row of sleeping bays used for grabbing some shuteye in zero-gee. Luca was zipped up in one of the bays. Scott hardly recognized her. She looked so much older than he remembered, even though the last visual communication they had had was only seven months ago.

"Is she sleeping?" Scott asked as he floated in closer to her. "Is she okay?"

"She's in a catatonic state, has been for a few days now."

"What happened out here, Steph? Where's Weismann, the captain?"

Steph let out a long sigh. "It's a long story, Scott. For starters, Weismann is dead, murdered by his own crew."

"What...dead? Who's piloting the ship?"

Steph pointed at the sleeping figure zipped up in the bay. "Luca. That's why I was stuck here—until you showed up."

"Since when did Luca know how to pilot a spacecraft?"

"Like I said, it's long story. Weismann's crew realized

there was a big payout for her, so they did away with the captain and were planning on handing us over to VanHeilding. Fortunately, we escaped. But neither of us could pilot a ship. That's when Luca started using a neural lace that Athena had given her to interface with the ship's data-stream. She figured it out and got us this far."

"But Luca hates anything to do with mind-machine interfaces. It freaks her out, literally."

"Yeah, well, she got pretty good at it. Until we ran out of food and water. So we took a chance on docking at this relay beacon. That's when they found us. Somehow, they took over the ship's systems so we couldn't undock."

"When was this?"

"Around two days ago. Luca managed to do her thing and release the ship, but...she never woke up. I've tried everything I can think of to revive her, but I have extremely limited medical resources here. We've just been floating out here ever since."

"Can she be moved?"

"Yes. Other than being somewhat malnourished and dehydrated, she's physical okay, as far as I can tell. It's just...like she simply doesn't want to wake up."

Scott removed his helmet and took a deep breath. "We need to get you out of here, and quick. They'll be coming soon, so we don't have much time. We should get back to New World One. It's the closest place with the best medical facilities."

"Is it true the QI on Ceres has been destroyed?" Steph asked as she began to unzip Luca from the sleeping bay.

"Yes. Unbelievable, isn't it? Who would have thought that was possible just a few months ago?"

"This shit's just got serious." She shook her head a little.

"It sure has. They destroyed it with a missile strike from orbit. VanHeilding has been using his Node Runners to hide the ship from the QIs. But now that Homer is gone, they're out in the open. Cyrus has been putting together some old-school tech to track the ship while keeping off-grid. So far, the ship hasn't moved—it's still in orbit around Ceres. But the feeling is that they're planning an attack on New World One."

"And you want to go back there?" Steph's eyes widened.

"It's fine, Steph. They've got a very good defense system that can blow that VanHeilding ship into atoms. Miranda should also there by the time we get back. And her ship, the Perception, is armed to the teeth. So all we have to do is get back there."

"Sounds like you're not sure about that."

Scott paused for a moment. "Look, this could be nothing, but Cyrus suspects there's another VanHeilding ship out here somewhere. That's why we need to get moving."

"Well, let's get going then." She jerked her head toward the airlock.

"You get whatever you need packed up. I'm going to

dock the two ships together so we can transfer without the need for EVA suits."

Scott looked back at the sleeping figure of Luca, reached out, and touched her arm. "It's okay, kiddo, we got you now." He turned to head for the airlock, but hesitated for a beat. "Eh...Luca didn't say anything to you about...battle droids?"

Steph's eyes widened. "Now you're beginning to freak me out. Battle droids? No. Why?"

Scott waved a hand. "Ah, it's probably nothing. Never mind."

24

RETURN

As Scott exited the orbit hopper's airlock and came back out into the vacuum of space, he couldn't help but scan the heavens looking for any telltale signs of a VanHeilding ship. Not that it was possible to spot anything unless it was right on top of him. But nonetheless, he had an uneasy feeling as he crossed the distance to his shuttle.

A short time later, he docked the two ships together and once he was satisfied that the connection was secure, he allowed both environments to equalize. Then he then took off the bulky EVA suit and opened the airlock between the two craft. Steph had already moved Luca out from her sleeping bay and now floated her through the airlocks. Between the two of them they gently transferred Luca into Scott's ship and strapped her securely to one of the passenger seats.

Steph was just about to fold herself into one of the

other seats when she stopped. "Wait, I forgot something. I need to go back and get it."

"What? Don't take too long, gotta get out of here as soon as possible."

She returned less than a minute later holding the small robotic drone.

"What's that thing?" Scott said as he shut the airlock door.

"It's a semi-autonomous drone, controlled by a neural lace. Athena built this for Luca. I think it was kind of a birthday present." She held it up so Scott could get a good look at it. "Without this, we never would have made it this far. It's what Luca used to control the ship."

Scott could tell from just a cursory look that this was clearly a sophisticated bit of tech. "Athena gave this to Luca knowing that using a neural lace sends her into a fit of panic?" Scott asked as he strapped himself into the pilot seat.

"Listen, Scott. There's something you should know about Luca, something that I've only begun to realize over the last few days."

Scott prepared to decouple the shuttle from the battered old orbit hopper. "What's that?"

"You know that her DNA had been...tweaked by the VanHeilding Corporation, back when Miranda was captive?"

"Yeah, so? Don't tell me she's gonna live for two hundred years?"

"No, not that. Although, she might. But we've been

monitoring her development over the years, keeping an eye out for any...anomalies. And for a long time, there didn't seem be anything out of the ordinary. Apart from maybe her hyper-sensitivity to electromagnetic energy. Yet what I've seen her do in the last few days leads me to believe that this hyper-sensitivity is a symptom of something deeper." She held up the drone again, examining it briefly. "This thing has a shard of the QI, Athena imbedded within it. Apparently, when Luca was interacting with the data-stream, it came online and it told her some things...things that Athena knew about her, or had suspected all along."

"Oh, what sort of things?"

"It told her that she was an experiment by VanHeilding to develop a next level Node Runner."

"Holy crap. How did Luca react to that?"

"Not very well, as you can imagine. But I think it answered a lot of questions she had about herself."

"Like what?"

"Oh, she said that she often felt dislocated from the real world, and this revelation seemed to resonate with her."

By now, Scott had detached the shuttle and slowly moved it out from the beacon. He was readying the ship for a burn to take them back to the New World. Steph tightened up her seat harness and braced herself for the burst of acceleration to come. But as she glanced back at Scott, she could see he was focused on the navigation screen. He tapped an icon to bring up the holo-display.

"I think we've got company." His finger pointed to a blip on the very edge of the schematic. "Big ship, heading our way." He glanced over at Steph. "Looks like Cyrus was right. Better buckle up. I'm going to try and outrun it, so this is going to be intense." He hit initiate and promptly passed out.

WHEN SCOTT RETURNED TO CONSCIOUSNESS, he found Steph's seat empty. The burn had completed and they were moving at close to top speed for this shuttle. But when he checked, he could see that the same ship he'd spotted near the beacon was not that far behind them. He was convinced now that it was clearly the second VanHeilding ship that Cyrus had alluded to. And there was no doubt in Scott's mind that it was chasing them down.

At their current speed, they would be back at New World One in less than eighteen hours. He unfastened his harness, floated out of the seat, and pulled himself through the companionway that led down into the main cabin of the shuttle. Steph was tending to a hydration pack attached Luca's right arm. It was like an old-school IV line except designed with a pressure pump for zero-gee. She glanced up at Scott as he entered.

"How is she?" Scott asked as he floated in beside her.

"She's okay, still the same. I was just making sure the hydration line didn't get screwed up during that burn.

You weren't joking about that kick. Did we lose that ship?"

"No, it's right behind us, definitely chasing us down. The only problem now is that we'll be coming in hot into the New World, bringing trouble with us. I need to get a message out to Cyrus and Miranda and let them know."

Steph simply nodded in reply.

He cast his gaze at Luca. Her face had regained some of its color; gone was the pallid complexion of earlier. Maybe there was a real chance she would come around.

"I should have been there for her." His voice was low.

"You're here now, Scott."

"I should never have let them talk me into sending her to Earth all those years ago."

"Maybe, but would you forgive yourself if something bad happened?"

Scott gave a slight nod. "No, I suppose not."

"Then don't beat yourself up over it. It is what it is. She's here now, and she needs you…and Miranda."

A brief moment passed, and Scott contemplated this. "Yeah, I suppose you're right." He bucked up a bit. "Anyway, I'd better go get that message sent."

He floated back to the flight deck, strapped himself in, and began to send a message over X-band.

"Miranda, Cyrus, this is Scott here. You'll be glad to hear I've located Luca and Steph, both are on board now and we're on our way back to the New World. However, Luca seems to be in some sort of catatonic state. According to Steph, she used a neural lace to interface with the beacon's network and ended up coming face-to-face with some of VanHeilding's Node Runners.

"However, we've got a bigger problem on our hands. You were right about that second ship, Cyrus, and it showed up at the beacon just as we were leaving. We now have it on our tail. I'm going to delay our retro-burn to the very last second to put some extra space between us and that ship. I hope you've got those defenses up and running, because we're going to need them."

25

BATTLE DROID

The ship chasing them down was still a few hours behind, But Scott was taking a big risk delaying the retro-burn until the last second. He wanted to arrive at the New World well ahead of the pursuers. But the longer he delayed the burn, the higher the thrust required to slow them down, and that meant heavy gee, which meant that he and Steph would probably black out.

Any time they would gain might well be nullified by how long it took them to regain consciousness after the burn. The doctor could handle it better than Scott—she always could—but she could not pilot the ship. Then there was the effect on Luca. That sort of physical strain could not be good for her. So in the end, he decided to take it slow and steady and hope that Cyrus had enough firepower to fend off the VanHeilding ship. He reckoned since they wanted Luca alive, they would not simply blow them to pieces. Nevertheless, he would need to get his timing right, and stay alert.

For the first hour of the retro-burn, he and Steph could do nothing except watch the main navigation monitor as the VanHeilding craft slowly gained on them. By the second hour, they began to get a visual image of it on the main monitor, albeit at maximum zoom. But by the end of the third hour, the ship was virtually snapping at their heels.

The retro-burn ended as suddenly as it had begun, and Scott could feel his body being released from the punishing gee-forces it had been subjected to, yet it took him a few moments to recover enough to even speak. "I'm getting too old for this shit."

"You and me both."

"You always seemed to be better able to handle this then anyone I know, Steph."

"Did I ever tell you? I hate space."

"Many times, Steph. Many times," he said as he hit the comms icon to contact Cyrus. But before he could establish a connection, Steph slapped him on the upper arm to get his attention and pointed at the main monitor.

"Look, Scott. Look! They're firing missiles at us."

Scott zoomed in on the display. Two stubby metallic objects were accelerating away from the underbelly of the VanHeilding ship. "They're not missiles, Steph. They're battle droids."

"Is that good or bad?"

"They're not trying to blow us to bits, so that's good.

They're trying to take control of this shuttle, and if they do, then that's bad." Scott hit the comms icon again and finally raised Cyrus.

"Scott, we have your ship on screen. And you've got two objects closing in on you fast. They look like droids of some kind."

"Please tell me those defenses are up and running, Cyrus."

"One of the weapons turrets is operational and could theoretically hit those droids."

"Theoretically?"

"They're not fully calibrated. Meaning that the plasma blast might not go where we want, and your ship is in the way of a clear shot."

"Okay, understood. I'll make some space for you, then you hit those bastards as hard as you can."

"You got it."

"I'm going to adjust our vector thirty degrees down from our current trajectory. When you see that happen, you'll have a window of opportunity, but only for a few seconds before they readjust their flight path."

"We're ready when you are."

"Okay. Wait for my mark."

Scott slowly reoriented the craft so it was again facing the direction of travel. Through the cockpit window, he could see the massive cylindrical habitat of New World One come into view, still some distance away. Then he dialed in the new vector. "Okay, Cyrus. Here we go."

He hit initiate and suddenly felt his body being

hauled upward from his seat; only the harness held him in place. As the craft dropped, he caught sight of two plasma blasts emanating from the New World, followed by two more in quick succession. They whipped past the shuttle at impressive speed, one coming perilously close, momentarily causing the cockpit controls to flicker as it passed.

"Holy crap, that was close." Steph glanced around the cockpit as the electronics settled down and stopped flickering.

Scott's attention was now on the rear monitor as he tracked the path of the four incandescent balls of plasma.

Two were well wide of the mark and sailed past the targets out into deep space. But the third was a direct hit. The droid flared briefly as it suffered catastrophic systems failure. It tumbled off in a spiral. But the fourth plasma bolt only grazed its target. For a moment, Scott and Steph held their breath, waiting to see if it had been close enough to effect enough damage on the droid. It didn't, and the machine kept on coming.

"Crap, they only hit one. They need to fire again!" Steph almost shouted at Scott.

"We don't have time—it's too close." He tried to shift the craft's vector again, but it was too slow to react.

Thump!

"Scott, Scott, it's on the hull!"

"I know, I know."

"What do we do?" Steph stared up at the cockpit roof with wide-eyed fear.

Scott's first thought was to do a high-acceleration burn and try to shake off the droid that way. But it would take them way out of range of the New World weapons system, where they would be easy prey for another salvo of battle droids.

"Scott?" The comms crackled into life.

"Cyrus. One down. But the other just attached itself to the hull."

"I see it. Listen, I've got a crazy idea. If you can get the craft closer, we can shoot you with a low-intensity blast."

"That's crazy, Cyrus. It will completely disable the ship, including life support."

"Yeah, I know. But you should have enough volume of air inside to last you for a while. We can get a ship out to you in twenty minutes."

"I don't know, Cyrus. From what little I remember about low-intensity plasma blasts, you could still blow a hole in our hull. That's game over."

"Got any EVA suits?"

"Just two, and they could also suffer electronic damage from the blast."

"I said it was a crazy idea, but it's all I got."

"Appreciate it, Cyrus. But let me try something else first."

"What?"

"No time to explain, that droid is on the move. Gotta go."

Scott killed the comms and unfastened his seat

harness. "Steph, I'm going outside to see if I can get rid of that droid."

"What? Are you nuts? That thing is probably armed to the teeth. You'll get yourself killed."

By now, Scott had floated out of the cockpit and down to the suit locker. "You heard what Cyrus was planning. It could kill us all."

Steph, who had followed Scott down into the main cabin, now grabbed his arm. "You don't have to do this."

Scott paused for a moment. "I'm sorry Steph...for getting you into all this shit. You don't deserve it."

"Yeah, well, it is what it is, and you know me well enough to know I'm not one to back out when the going gets tough. But what you're doing is crazy—taking on a battle droid?"

Scott started getting suited up. "Any minute now, this ship will be under VanHeilding control. That means we're all screwed."

Scott clipped his helmet on and shoved a plasma pistol into a side cargo pocket. He gave Steph a wry smile and stepped into the airlock. "Just like old times, eh?" The inner door closed before Steph could answer.

SCOTT ATTACHED the tether just as the outer door opened, presenting the vastness of space before him. It was a moment that never failed to invoke a sense of awe, and probably the very reason he had hitched his future to a life amongst the stars. Perhaps it was the romantic in him, yet romantics seldom have a good end. More often than not they end in tragedy. Yet, he only had one thought in his mind—bring Luca back to safety and maybe have a chance to make up for all these lost years, assuming he made it out of this alive. He opened a comms channel to Steph.

"Where's the droid now?"

"Top side, back near the starboard engine bay, around ten meters from the airlock."

"Okay, keep me posted if and when it moves."

Scott took out his weapon and slowly raised his head out of the airlock. He could see the machine, just where Steph said it would be. A quadruped, with a gait that was a cross between a big cat for speed, and an ape for dexterity. Yet it was moving uncharacteristically slow. Then he realized that it needed to use the handholds just like a human would, otherwise it would float away from the hull and have to use its thrusters to get back. It was currently working its way to the rear of the craft, where all the main ship systems where housed.

Scott gently raised his weapon, got the target firmly in its sights, and fired. An incandescent blue ball of electrical rage hit the droid on its left flank and it seemed to lose its grip on the ship's hull. But as Scott moved fully out of the airlock, he could see that the droid was still clinging on, and still functioning. He had only inflicted minor damage on it. For a brief second, he checked the weapon, looking for some reason as to why it hadn't blown a hole in the droid. Yet there was nothing wrong with it; the machine was simply made of stronger stuff than he had reckoned.

By now, he was fully in view of the droid that had quickly reoriented itself to seek out the source of the attack. Scott, realizing that he had left himself exposed, frantically tried to gain cover back inside the airlock. But he was not fast enough, and the droid returned fire.

The blast fell short, hitting the hull just in front of him. But Scott lost his grip on the handhold as he twisted to avoid the impact, and now he found himself tumbling in free space, with nothing but the tether connecting him to the ship. Another blast whipped past him.

He fired back, but it was wild and random, only aiming in the general direction of the droid. This also spun him around more and more as the kickback added to his erratic momentum—which was probably the only thing that prevented the droid from scoring a direct hit on him.

Scott needed to do something, and fast. He fired a blast above his head, which propelled him downward until the tether jerked at its full extension. He then spun around the underside of the shuttle, slamming into the hull and began frantically grabbing at anything that even approximated a hand hold, finally gaining purchase on a sensor array.

"Scott?"

"A little busy right now, Steph."

"So I see. The droid's on the move, heading around to you. You'd better get outta there."

"Which way's it coming?"

"Directly behind you."

"Okay, keep me posted on what it's doing."

"You got it."

Scott scrambled forward only to be halted by a tug on the fully extended tether. "Shit."

"What's wrong?"

"Tether. I need to lose it."

"You'd better hurry."

Scott unclipped the tether and began to work his way forward across the shuttle's undercarriage. *This was not the way it was supposed to go,* he thought. Not only did he have an ineffective weapon, he was now on the run from this thing, and in peril of losing a hand hold and floating off into space.

"Steph?"

"Still here."

"I have an idea. Do you know how to initiate a burn?"

"Damnit Scott, I'm a doctor, not a pilot."

"Get on with Cyrus—it's his ship, he'll talk you through it. Tell him I need a five-second, low-thrust burn —and hurry."

FOR THE NEXT minute or so, Scott played hide and seek with the droid. It was not as agile as him, so he could keep one step ahead of it. But what it lacked in agility it made up for in its sheer determination to kill him, and he had a few near misses. He wouldn't be able to keep this up indefinitely.

"Scott, I think I have it figured out."

"Good. Now listen carefully. I'm going to lure this droid out to the rear of the shuttle and around the starboard engine exhaust port. When I give you the signal, you initiate the burn. I'm hoping it will be enough to vaporize this thing."

There was a momentary pause.

"Steph, did you get that?"

"Yeah, but you can't be out there, Scott. You'll get thrown off the hull, you'll never be able to hang on. That much I do know."

"Don't worry about me, I'll reconnect to the tether, that will keep me from floating away."

"But that might not take the strain. It'll snap."

"Well, that's a risk I'm willing to take, Steph. So just wait for my signal."

"But this is crazy, Scott."

"Of course it is. Just be ready."

SCOTT PLANNED the course he would take in his mind. He needed the droid in the direct line of fire when the engines ignited, and for him to be hooked back onto the tether. But no matter which way he worked it in his mind, there would be a moment when he could be wide open for a kill shot. But he had no other choice.

He slowly clambered his way along the underside of

the shuttle and had just reached the engine bay when the droid finally came into view behind him. It unleashed a blast that flew past his feet as he pulled himself up into the starboard exhaust cowling. He hung there for a moment, waiting for the droid to come out from the underside of the ship, but it was a no-show.

"Steph, can you see where the droid is?"

"It's on the undercarriage, down near the starboard engine bay."

"Is it moving?"

"Nope, just squatting there. No, wait... I think it's doing something to the hull. It looks like it's opening some panel or other."

"Crap. I think it's given up chasing me and going back to plan A."

"So what now?"

"I need to get it angry." Scott leaned around the edge of the cowling and took aim at the droid. He fired off three shots, two of which hit, to little effect other than to get its attention. He ducked back just in time as the droid returned fire, but still it didn't follow.

Scott leaned out again and discharged the entire weapon at the droid. This time it had the desired effect: it got angry and unleashed a barrage of return fire. Scott, in the meantime, had clambered out of the way.

"It's moving, Scott."

"Okay, get ready to initiate that burn." He moved fast over the face of the exhaust cowling around to the topside of the ship. He could see the tether floating out from the airlock. He would either have to make it all the way to the airlock or take a leap of faith and launch himself off the hull and try and grab the floating tether before he went tumbling out into space.

He glanced behind him to see one of the droid's forelimbs coming over the rim of the cowling.

Screw it—it's now or never, he thought, and launched himself at the tail end of the tether. He frantically grabbed at it, but it bounced off his hand. He tried again with the other with no better luck. On the third try, he finally managed to snag it and started pulling it in to get to the clip end. Below him, the droid was directly over the engine exhaust but maneuvering itself to take aim. He felt the end clip onto the tether and snapped it onto his EVA suit.

"Hit it, Steph. Do it now, NOW!"

The engines ignited, and he was slammed back down against the hull as the shuttle accelerated. A plasma blast whizzed past his head. He craned his neck against the forces trying to rip him from the ship and looked back at the starboard engine. Both of the droid's forelimbs were fanatically scrambling at the edge of the cowling, trying to gain purchase while the rest of the machine was engulfed in a fiery plasma plume extending some several meters. He saw it finally lose its battle and succumb to the white-hot maelstrom—an incandescent ball tumbling backward out into space.

At the same time, Scott felt like his limbs were about

to be torn from his body, such were the forces he was being subjected to.

"Kill it, Steph...kill it."

The burn ceased as quickly as it started, and the acceleration eased. Slowly, with much pain and effort, Scott clawed his way back to the airlock and closed the outer door.

∾

WHEN SCOTT's shuttle finally docked at New World One, he was understandably relieved to have made it back with all on board still in one piece. However, now that the Perception had also arrived, it would be the first time in years that he would meet Miranda face to face.

It was a prospect that he was both excited for and dreading in equal measure. They had grown apart over many years—not because his feelings were any less, but that Miranda reminded him of the trauma of Luca's exile. And perhaps, if he was being truthful with himself, a small part of him blamed Miranda for that. But it was not her fault either, and he knew she felt exactly the same loss—she had a different way of dealing with it. All these feelings came flooding back as the shuttle came into dock.

It also didn't help that she would look almost exactly the same as he remembered her twenty years ago, by virtue of her enhanced DNA. She would still look thirty, while he, being a mere mortal, felt every one of the fifty years now resting on his shoulders.

Yet they had been in constant contact over the last few weeks, not direct conversations as such, because the vast distances of space provided no such luxuries. But still, they had exchanged more words the last three weeks than they had in the last ten years. Yet they were curt, short, professional. More like updates on progress than inquiries about each other's personal well-being. But even so, there was no escaping the subtext in their stilted dialogue—they both needed each other, and they both knew it.

When they did finally meet, their moment was overtaken by both Miranda's joy at having found Luca, followed by deep concern over her current physical state. As they made their way to the med-bay, Scott was overcome with a deep desire to wrap Miranda up in his arms and tell her everything would be alright. He resisted; now was not the time. But maybe there would be another.

26

AWAKENING

Somewhere in the back of Luca's mind, she was aware of the need to return to the physical world. The ship would be free of the beacon by now, but it would still need her input to pilot it to New World One. Part of her had sensed the presence of another VanHeilding ship in close proximity, so they were not out of the woods yet. She had gotten a hint of it from the mind of the Node Runner. But how far away it was, she was not sure. Nevertheless, it was best for her to return and get the ship moving again.

She expected to return to the familiar landscape of the ship's flight deck. But as she probed, she realized that she had lost the interface connection—Fly was gone, or offline, or worse. A sting of panic pierced her mind as she began to decipher the physical stimuli now entering her consciousness. Her body felt like stone, her limbs like leaden weights struggling to respond to her desire to move. Bright light flooded into her optic nerves as she began to open her eyes—just a little at first, until she regained some control over her limbs and raised a hand to shield them from the glare. *Where the hell am I?* she thought.

Her vision slowly adjusted, bringing details of her surroundings into focus. She expected to see the cockpit of the ship, but instead she was looking at...a celling. Bright, white, clean, almost sterile in its appearance. She was lying flat on her back looking up, and she was somewhere with full gravity—that's why she found it so hard to move. It was definitely not inside the relay beacon, since that had no artificial gravity.

Have I been captured? Is this a VanHeilding ship? These thoughts flickered through her mind as she tried to compute the parameters of her current location. Panic began to fuel her body and she summoned the effort to turn sideways, raising herself up on one elbow. She was not tied down, not trapped, free to move. This was a good sign.

Luca scanned the room, and judging by the other beds, all of which were empty, and the equipment that was arrayed around the room, it was a med-bay. But where? And how did she get here, considering that only a few short moments ago she was sitting in the pilot seat on board the banged-up orbit hopper and interfaced with the Grid.

Something tugged at her arm. An IV line snaked into a vein just above her wrist. Luca's gut reaction was to rip it out, but she halted and instead followed the transparent plastic tubing all the way up to a pouch suspended from a hook containing a clear liquid, labeled *NaCl 0.9%*. She knew enough to know that this was a *saline solution*, common for a patient suffering from dehydration. In other words—harmless.

Her eyes returned to where the IV entered her body just above the wrist and began to peel off the plaster covering the cannula. Then she gently pulled out the long, thin plastic needle. Blood began to pool at the insertion point, and she held a finger over it to stanch the flow. At the very same moment, the door opened and in walked Dr. Stephanie Rayman. "Luca, you're awake."

Luca took a second to respond. "Steph?" her voice was faint, her throat parched. She took the finger off her wrist and began to rub her neck.

"It's okay, take it easy, Luca. You shouldn't take that out, you're still dehydrated. Here, drink this." Steph handed her a beaker of water. Luca sipped, the clear cold liquid soothing her fragile throat, so she drank and drank until it was empty, then held out the beaker for Steph to refill it.

"We thought you would never wake up. You've been out for days."

Luca felt her throat loosen. "What happened? Where am I?"

"We're in the New World. We arrived around fourteen hours ago. You were catatonic, as well as malnourished and dehydrated. I got some fluids and nutrients into you and...well, it seems to have done the trick."

"But how? I was just—"

"Better rest. We can explain later."

Luca resigned herself to Steph's medical advice, primarily because her throat still felt like sand, and she began to gulp down another beaker of water. She was halfway into it when the door opened again. This time, Scott and Miranda entered.

"Luca!" Her mother was the first to rush over. "You're awake."

Luca nodded. "Yeah."

Miranda wrapped her up in her arms. "I'm so glad you're awake." She squeezed her tight for a moment before releasing her, sitting back on the bed as she did. "I'm sorry...for all the crap we put you through. It was stupid, reckless...shouldn't have made you leave Earth." She glanced up at Scott as if to seek confirmation.

"You had us worried," was the most he could add.

Luca began to feel those large gaps she had always had in her emotional fabric finally fill up and close over. Here they all were, after all these years and all that she had been through, together again at last. Yet another part of her felt a little anticlimactic, and what she had sought at the outset of her journey was now replaced with a new set of emotional gaps. Not least, how she got here. "Can someone please tell me what the hell is going on?"

"Your ship was dead in the water, floating free near

Beacon 23. Scott took a shuttle and rescued you." Miranda put her hand on Scott's arm.

"Dead in the water?" Luca searched her mind for any memory of this, but there was none.

"Yes, you were out for the count, and Steph couldn't pilot the ship."

Luca was sitting up now and looked from one to the other. "I was interfaced with the Grid...just now...a few moments ago. How can I be here?"

Since no one had a good answer to this, they all stood in silence for a beat. Then Luca reached up to the back of her skull and touched the neural lace; it was still active and fully meshed around her cranium. "Fly—where's Fly? I can't sense it."

"The drone?" Miranda again looked up at Scott.

"Yes, the one Athena gave me. Where is it?"

"It's here." Steph picked up Luca's backpack, reached in, and pulled out the drone. "It's deactivated. That's why you can't sense it."

Luca gave a long sigh. "Sorry, I'm just a little... confused at the moment, still trying to process it all."

"That's okay, Luca." Miranda leaned in and placed a hand on Luca's shoulder. "Just rest, you're safe now."

Luca shook her head. "We're not safe here, they're coming. Droids, hundreds of them."

Scott, Miranda, and Steph all exchanged glances. The type reserved for when discussing crazy people.

"I've seen them, row upon row, ready to be deployed."

"How do you know this?" said Scott, a look of concern developing across his features.

"The neural lace Athena gave me." She touched the back of her head again—a little troubled by the fact that the lace had not deactivated. "I used it to interface with Fly, the drone. And through that to connect to the ship's systems and control the craft until we docked with the beacon. That's when we were hacked...by Node Runners. They disabled the release mechanism so we couldn't leave. So I just followed the data-stream all the way to the source."

Luca paused to look up at them. "I read his mind, the Runner. He was afraid...afraid of what I might do to him —I think." Luca's eyes widened, and she shook her head a little. "I probed his mind. There were images of a drone army in the cargo hold of a big ship, or maybe more than one ship, I'm not sure. There were other things too, things I could not understand. But he was in such fear of me that I withdrew back along the data-stream. Last thing I remember was sending you a message with the images and undocking the ship, then...I woke up here." She gave a gesture at the room.

This was met with silence, and Luca suspected that they were all, in their own individual ways, considering her sanity.

"Don't you see? It's an invading army, and the New World is the target. They are coming. VanHeilding and the other Earth families are coming to take control."

"They're already here, Luca," Scott said matter-of-factly.

She sat bolt upright, her body already regaining some sense of balance in the natural environment of full gravity. "Here, now?"

"Two ships of the Seven, parked way out from the habitat. Out of range of our plasma cannons—waiting. The largest of the two was responsible for the destruction of QI, Homer on Ceres. The second, smaller ship chased us back from the relay beacon. It deployed two battle drones that attacked us en route. But we...dealt with them and got here in one piece." Scott gave a dismissive gesture as if to imply it had all been just a minor inconvenience.

"Are you sure about what you saw?" Miranda leaned in a little, her voice low and maternal. "Could it have been just...a dream?"

Anger welled up inside Luca. How could her mother say this to her, after all the she had already hidden from her? "You know it's not a dream or some figment of my imagination. You knew all along I had been engineered from birth to be some sort of monster designed to navigate the data-stream, like a biological QI—but you never thought to tell me."

For the third time in as many minutes, there was silence in the room before Miranda finally answered. Her voice was low and maternal. "It wasn't like that, Luca. At the start, we didn't even know. Only after the kidnapping attempts were made did we start to wonder why. It broke our hearts to send you away to live on Earth. But we just wanted you to be safe."

"You mean to be a lab rat? To be studied by Athena, and Dr. Rayman, and her institute?"

"I'm sorry," Miranda said, with a hint of resignation in her voice. "I know we should have told you, but...there never seemed to be a right time. We just wanted to protect you."

Luca lay back against the headboard and let out a long sigh. She looked at the concern on her parents' faces and slowly began to realize that she was no longer angry any more. It all seemed vaguely distant and unimportant. "It's okay, really. I get it. Why put me through it."

"Yes, yes, exactly." Scott seized his moment to contribute.

"It may seem strange, but I'm alright with it. For the first time in my life, it all makes sense." Luca looked up, astonished to see a tear rolling down her mother's cheek, even her father's outer shell seemed to be cracking. He held his hand up to his temple, his head lowered. Then Luca realized that he was receiving a message from someone. He glanced back at her, a little embarrassed to find her looking at him with what she could only assume he interpreted as a disapproving look.

"What is it?" Miranda had noticed the concern on Scott's face.

"They've just issued an ultimatum. Hand over control of New World One, or they'll take it by force."

27

DECISION TIME

Under Dr. Rayman's insistence, they decamped to an anti-room with a long observation window used by medical staff to keep an eye on patients. Luca needed to recuperate, and Scott and Miranda talking incessantly to her was not going to help. So in true doctor style, Steph kicked them all out so Luca could get some rest.

Cyrus found time to join them after the news of the ultimatum had been issued, seemingly to reassure them that it was all just a bluff.

"We should get out now, before it all goes to rat-shit." Steph sat back in a soft low seat. She looked drained; the journey here had taken a toll on her, and what she really needed was some rest.

"No. They're bluffing. There's no way they can get past our defenses. We've got two long-range plasma cannon turrets fully operational. A single blast would be enough to stop either of those VanHeilding ships dead in their tracks. We could turn them into a dust cloud if we wanted to." Cyrus seemed genuinely proud of the New World's weapons capability and delivered his reply with wild, enthusiastic gesticulations.

"What about this *vision* of Luca's?" Miranda directed her question to Cyrus.

"You mean the droids in the image files?"

"Yeah. What if it's real? That would change the equation."

"I don't see how it changes anything." Cyrus was still convinced of the New World's weapons system. "We destroyed the droid that was chasing you down from the relay beacon. Even if they have more of them, they're still no match for a plasma cannon."

"But Luca's talking hundreds." Scott, having had first-hand experience fighting one of these droids, did not share Cyrus's confidence. "Could we really defend against that?"

"We don't really know what she saw, or what she thought she saw. It could be anything, or nothing. You can't make a decision based on *visions*." Miranda did air quotes with her fingers. "Think about it, she's been catatonic for several days. Who knows what dreams she's been having? It's not reality."

"I know what I saw, and it's real," said a strange voice from out of nowhere.

"What the..." Scott looked around for the source, as did the others.

"We're not safe here. We need to get out," the voice continued.

Scott finally located the source. The drone, Fly, was resting on the edge of a countertop just inside the door. He never noticed it coming in, and presumably none of the others did either. "Luca?"

"Yes."

He stood up and looked through the observation window back into the ward. Luca was sitting up in bed, arms folded over her chest, a deep scowl on her face.

"Eh, did you hear all that?" Miranda joined Scott at the window.

"I did." Fly lifted off the counter, flew a little closer to the group, and landed back down again.

"Luca"—Steph stood up and peered out through the window—"you need to get some rest."

Luca just scowled back.

"Are you...controlling that thing?" Miranda turned around and directed her question toward Fly.

"Yes, it's proved very useful. We wouldn't have got here without it."

"Holy crap." Cyrus moved over and started to examine the drone. "This is a very elegant bit of engineering. Very cool." He turned his attention to Scott and tapped his temple. "I've been extolling the virtues of the mind-machine interface to Scott for ages. But he just doesn't get it."

"Yeah, well, maybe I like my brain too much."

Miranda raised a hand to silence everyone for a

moment; her demeanor became serious. "Okay, let's say you're right, Luca, and there's a ship, or maybe two ships full of these battle droids. How long would they take the to reach here, Cyrus?"

"Eh, well, they wouldn't. We'd just blow them to bits before they got anywhere near us."

"Assume that some could get through. What's the travel time?" Miranda persisted.

"Fifteen minutes, give or take." He wobbled his hand to emphasize his approximation.

"And how long for us to get to the shuttle dock?"

Scott suddenly saw where Miranda was going with this. "At least thirty minutes."

"Anyone else see a problem here?"

Scott nodded. "If we have to get out in a hurry, it could mean fighting our way off this tub."

"But there would need to be swarms of droids to get some past the defenses." Cyrus was not giving up just yet.

"There are. I'm sure of it," said Fly/Luca.

Miranda turned to Cyrus. "Got any heavy weapons stashed on the New World?"

"Eh...not really. Just the usual small arms, that's about it."

Miranda unclipped her plasma pistol and held it up. "So you're saying this is all we have to fight our way off?"

"Hey, New World One represents the pinnacle of human civilization." Cyrus gesticulated wildly. "Look around you, it's a goddamn utopia—we don't need guns here."

"Well, that's just great! So now that we're in paradise, we're reduced to throwing rocks at our enemies?" Miranda said, a little cynically.

"We don't have any of those, either."

"Will you two just cut it out." Steph stood up, looking from one to the other. "I didn't sign up for this crap. All I was supposed to do was to see that Luca got to Johnston, not go on a wild death-race across half the solar system."

"I'm sorry, Steph. Sorry you got dragged into this mess," Miranda replied apologetically.

"Yeah, well. The bottom line is what are we going to do now? Stay and hope for the best, or run away."

"Run away," said Fly/Luca.

"We've still got seven hours to decide," Cyrus reminded them.

"Even so, if we were to *run away*, then where to? Where do we go?" Scott sat down again.

"Somewhere there's a QI," said Miranda. "That's the only thing that can give us some protection."

"Yeah, but for how long?" said Scott. "If they can destroy the QI, Homer on Ceres, who's to say they can't do the same to any of the others?"

"Well, I want to get back to Earth," said Steph. "I hate space."

"Mars is on the far side of the sun. It would take months to get there," said Miranda. "Which leaves Europa, and the QI, Solomon. That's the closest to us, but they're so weird there, they give me the heebie-jeebies. I suggest we get to the Perception and then we can decide where best to go."

"Well, I'm going back to Earth, one way or the other," said Steph. "So, if it's okay with you guys, I'll be on the next transport heading that way."

Scott nodded his acceptance of Steph's desire to get back home. She had already gone beyond anything he or Miranda had asked of her. "I don't know how we can ever repay you for this, Steph."

"Well, you owe me one. Someday, I'll need something —that's when you can repay me."

"Of course, Steph. Anything," said Miranda.

"So we're getting out of here?" Fly buzzed its wings to get their attention.

"Luca, I'm not talking to you through that thing."

Fly buzzed its wings again. "We're not safe here. We need to go."

Miranda stood up and nodded. "Okay, decision time. Who's coming, who's staying. Cyrus, Steph?"

Cyrus shook his head. "No way I'm leaving. We're perfectly safe here. Nothing is going to get through."

"Seriously, Cyrus, if what Luca is saying is true, then then there's every possibility that the New World will be taken over by VanHeilding and his sponsors. And what do you think is going to happen to you when he realizes who you are, Cyrus Sanato, Chief Engineer of the Hermes, one of the people responsible for enabling the dominion of the QIs?"

Cyrus looked down at his feet and pursed his lips.

"Everything I have is here. Everything I've built is contained within this vast cylinder. I'm not leaving it. I'll take my chances here."

"Steph?"

"I need to return to Earth. I need to get back home."

Scott looked over at Cyrus. "There must be a ship heading for Earth, something with room for Steph?"

But the engineer was distracted. He had one hand on his right temple and seemed to be concentrating.

"Cyrus, what is it?"

The others detected Scott's concern and looked over at Cyrus, waiting for him to respond.

"Cyrus?"

He held a hand out to signal to them to be quiet for a moment as he focused. Scott, Miranda, and Steph all exchanged concerned glances. Even Fly/Luca twitched and buzzed its wings.

"Everything okay?" Scott said this more in hope than as a request for information.

Cyrus slowly turned his head toward him and the color drained from his face. "No—far from it. Everything just got real."

"What do you mean? What's going on?"

But Cyrus didn't answer. Instead, he rushed across the med-lab to a bank of monitors that occupied most of one wall, the others following after him.

"Cyrus." Scott grabbed the engineer's arm to get his attention. "What the hell is going on?"

"It's started."

"What has?"

"Luca's right—look." The large central monitor blossomed into life and displayed a view of space, black and empty. The image zoomed and zoomed again to pick out the brooding form of the main VanHeilding ship. Cyrus tapped at a control interface, and the image focused. Then they could see it: a mass of autonomous battle droids spewing out from the belly of the ship.

"Oh shit."

The image on the screen flipped to black empty space again, and then began zooming in on the second VanHeilding ship. It was the same—a mass of droids being ejected into space.

Miranda grabbed Scott's arm. "We gotta go, we can't stay here."

"Yeah, okay. Let's start making our way to the shuttle."

"I told you so." Fly swooped down onto one edge of the main monitor.

"And I told you, I'm not talking to you through that thing, Luca."

"Well, I'm stuck in this bed, under doctor's orders and tied down with tubes and wires."

Miranda screwed her mouth up. "Steph, what do you want to do?"

She glanced at Scott, and then her focus was drawn back to the monitor. On screen they could see the New World defense systems had started firing. Brief, sporadic trails of incandescent blue plasma raced across the space between, intercepting the droids, picking them off one at a time.

Cyrus punched the air. "Die, you bastards, die." His joy sent a ripple of elation through Scott's spine. But it was short-lived. As they watched, it became clear that the rate of fire was having little overall impact on the numbers heading their way.

"Can't it fire any faster?" Miranda asked.

"Have you got any idea how much energy it takes to create a blast of that magnitude?"

"So you're saying no."

For a moment, Cyrus didn't respond, but then he began to slowly shake his head. "Nobody thought we would need close-range weapons. This was designed as a deterrent to ships, not hordes of droids." He gestured at the screen and then visibly slumped down in a seat. "It's no good, there's just too many." He took his gaze away from the drama unfolding on the monitor and looked at Scott, Miranda, and Steph. "We're screwed."

28

OPERATION DROID

Scott had to hand it to VanHeilding and the other six Earth families who were funding this operation. It was a master stroke. By taking out the QI on Ceres, they now had free reign throughout this sector of the asteroid belt. But more than that, once the Seven had secured the Belt's primary resources, they would be able to exert considerable leverage over both Earth and Mars. The era of the QIs was ending, and a new order was beginning: messier, more violent, more human.

Now, with the aid of a few hundred semi-autonomous battle droids, there was nothing anyone could do to stop them taking over New World One. Even though the newly installed defense systems were busy trying to pick off as many of the incoming machines as possible, it was like trying to swat a swarm of killer bees by throwing a box of crayons at them. They might get a few, but

ultimately nowhere near enough to make a difference—
the two exterior plasma cannon arrays simply didn't have
the fire rate.

And even though some of the citizens were prepared
to stand and fight, they possessed no military training
and few effective weapons to combat such a formidable
mechanized foe. This fatal flaw in defense planning was
simply because no one had ever imagined such weapons
or personnel would be needed. Over two decades of
peace and stability will do that to a society—it was just
not seen as a priority.

The only force with any bite to take on these droids
were Miranda's cohort of mercenaries. They had the
training and the weapons. But there were only nine of
them in total, and only three of them were here on the
New World with Miranda. And they knew a losing battle
when they saw it. There was no way they could win this
one; it would be suicide. It was time to get out—and get
out now, before it was too late. Miranda sent them ahead
to get the shuttle ready while she and Steph got Luca up
and moving. Scott, for his part, tried to persuade Cyrus to
come with them.

"So you're leaving?" Cyrus said, not with any hint of
disappointment, more as a statement of fact.

"What choice do we have, Cyrus? Soon this place
will be under the control of the Seven, and there's
nothing anyone can do to stop that now. What do you
think will happen to us, and especially Luca, if we
stay?"

"I understand, Scott. You need to get out. But I'm staying."

"Cyrus, if you stay, you run the risk of VanHeilding finding out who you really are. And he's not going to forget those people responsible for his downfall all those years ago."

"I know, but everything I have, everything I've built in the last two decades, is here. If I leave, I lose it all."

"You could lose your life, Cyrus."

"It's a risk I'm willing to take, Scott. Weirdly, staying here is my way of fighting back."

"Cyrus, I hate leaving you here."

"I'll be fine. It's a vast habitat, and I know every inch of it. Plenty of places to hide if things get sketchy."

"Okay, but..."

"No buts, just go. You've got a brief window of opportunity. Once those droids get here, their first priority will be to find a way to reconnect the New World systems with the Grid. As soon as that happens, the Node Runners will have complete control—shuttle exit from the dock will probably be disabled."

"Anything you can do to override them?"

"I doubt it. Even I can't fight off a concerted data attack by a group of Node Runners, that's way too weird for me."

"Okay. Well, stay safe, old buddy. See you on the other side."

"Yeah, it'll be a story to tell the grandkids."

"I'll tell that to Luca."

~

THEY TRAVELED the three or so kilometers to the nearest elevator for the dock by commandeering one of the autonomous vehicles parked outside the med-lab. Luca was still very weak and operating on a cocktail of drugs that Steph had pumped into her. Even so, she insisted on interfacing with Fly, her drone. It hovered above them, providing some useful reconnaissance of the route ahead.

They exited the vehicle near the elevators as a great mass of people bunched together to get through the entrance bottleneck. There were other elevators they could use, but these were at least another two kilometers further along the rim, so they stuck with trying to get to the shuttle dock using this route.

It would take them up to an inner cylinder that housed the smaller shuttle craft in a fully pressurized, half-gee environment, so no need for EVA suits. But after that things might get trickier, as the shuttle would then have to navigate its way through a complex series of airlocks before being released out into space. Scott was getting anxious; time was passing, and they were making slow progress.

"This is crazy, we're never going to make it."

"We've got to. This is the fastest way off this habitat." Miranda pushed her way past a knot of people who didn't have quite the same sense of urgency about them. "Luca, what can you see up ahead?"

"People, lots of them. And they don't seem to be moving."

Scott glanced up at Fly, which had risen up some ten meters above them and had a clear view of all entrances. "Should we head for the other sector?"

"No way, that would slow us down even more. Just keep tight. I'll get us through here." Miranda unholstered her plasma weapon and with a considerable amount of pushing and shoving, and shouts of *clear the way, emergency, move it, asshole,* she barged a way through to an open elevator.

Fly swooped down and anchored itself onto Luca's right shoulder as they piled in and the doors shut. There were an anxious few minutes as the elevator traveled the two kilometers all the way up to the dock. As they ascended, gravity began to lessen slightly. Everyone made sure they were holding onto something before the elevator came to a halt, otherwise they would be lifted off the floor by its momentum. It spat them out onto the main dock concourse, which was busy with panicked people making their way to whatever craft would get them off the New World.

They were hurrying across this concourse to their shuttle's location when Scott's comms burst into life.

"Scott, Cyrus here. I've changed my mind, I'm coming with you."

"What, now?"

"I'm on my way to you, be there as soon as I can."

"What about all that...*everything I have is here* stuff?"

"Yeah, well it seems everything I have is leaving—bastards. After all I've done for them. None of my partners in this business want to stay here and stick it out. They're all running away and leaving me here swinging my tail."

"We're on the concourse, nearly at the ship, so you'd better get a move on. Where are you?"

"I'm close, taking an alternative route through the maintenance tunnels, a lot less traffic."

"How's the outer dock looking?"

"Multiple droids streaming in. But I get the impression they're not looking for a major fight—maybe they see killing contractors as bad for recruitment. After all, when they do take over, they're going to need these workers. The primary objective as I see it is to stop people leaving by blocking the main access routes. But there's been a new development. We've spotted several troop transports on their way. We'll soon have boots on the ground."

"They're not leaving anything to chance, are they?"

"No, and from what I'm seeing, no one's getting off this habitat without a fight, so I sincerely hope Miranda has stashed a load of weapons on that shuttle of hers."

"You know her so well, Cyrus."

"Oh crap..." The comms suddenly went dead.

"Cyrus, Cyrus?" Nothing. "Goddamnit, Cyrus?"

"What's going on?" Miranda called over to Scott as they arrived at the shuttle. The main airlock door was open with two of her crew standing guard in case anyone tried to commandeer the craft.

"We gotta wait. Cyrus has changed his mind, he's heading out with us."

"Well, where is he? We can't hang around." Miranda mounted the steps to the airlock.

"Cyrus is coming with us?" Steph grabbed Scott's arm.

"Seems he's finding out who his real friends are," said Scott as he stood at the airlock steps and scanned the concourse for any sign of the engineer.

"Droids, three of them, coming in through the floor." Luca was standing beside him, and had that thousand-yard stare people who are interfacing with a machine usually have. She was seeing all this through the drone's eyes.

"Where the hell is Cyrus? I thought you said he was on his way." Miranda poked her head out from the airlock door, but this time she was armed with a far superior weapon than her standard plasma pistol.

"He was, then the comms went dead."

"We gotta go, Scott," Miranda called out.

"Just give it another minute."

"We don't have a minute. If there are droids entering the dock, then it's not going to take them long to disable all the exit routes."

"Thirty seconds, then." He tapped his comms. "Cyrus, are you there? Come on buddy, don't do this to me." Still no response.

He glanced up and saw Fly heading toward the shuttle. *Luca must be bringing it back, he thought.*

He turned around and called over to her. "Luca, any sign of Cyrus?"

"No, just more droids."

Whomp!

Scott and Miranda instinctively ducked and looked around for the source of the distinctive sound of a heavy plasma weapon being discarded.

"There, look." Miranda pointed across to a large industrial transport ship. The rear ramp was down, and at its base three people were firing on an approaching droid. This got the attention of several other machines and they began converging in on the action.

"Shit, we've got multiple droids heading our way. We can't wait any longer. Get inside now, we're going." Miranda's voice was charged with urgency.

Scott looked around to see three droids and what looked like an android heading in their direction. The group were around a hundred meters away. Steph grabbed Luca by the arm and pulled her gently back toward the shuttle airlock. "We've run out of time. Miranda's right, we gotta go, Scott."

They backed up, at the same time constantly scanning the area for any sign of Cyrus, until all of them were inside the airlock. Scott took one last look, and with a deep sigh of resignation he hit the button to close the outer door.

Miranda was in the pilot seat, working the controls for the exit protocols. "Okay, let's get the hell out of here."

"Wait, look!" Scott pointed out the cockpit window. Cyrus was running across the concourse as fast as Scott had ever seen him move. The only problem was several droids were converging on him.

"He's not going to make it," said Miranda.

Scott remained silent for a beat. Miranda was right—the engineer was a goner.

The cockpit console pinged an alert to say the airlock had been activated. "What the hell? Someone's in the airlock."

Scott spun around to check. "Luca!"

Then they saw her, outside on the concourse moving toward Cyrus and the machines that pursued him. Fly buzzed overhead.

"What the hell is she doing? She's going to get herself killed."

29

EXODUS

L uca guided Fly high up over the concourse and took in the scene below. At least a dozen battle droids had infiltrated the area along with several androids that seemed to be central to coordinating the attack.

To her left, a battle was in progress, although it was more of a skirmish at this point. The two contractors from the transport ship, who had started firing on the battle droids, were lying in heaps on the floor. One droid was currently making its way up the rear loading ramp of the ship, directing fire into the interior as it moved. Luca could hear the screams.

To her right, another futile skirmish was taking place, with a similar outcome. Elsewhere, transports were being boarded by panicked citizens, while luckier ones were in the process of departing.

All this she established in an instant. But her main

focus was on the group of machines that now surrounded Cyrus. Fly dropped lower, hovering directly above the trapped engineer. He had the look of a frightened animal, with one hand held out in front of him, while the other rested on his right temple. He was interfacing with something, Luca could sense. He was trying in his own feeble way to assess the situation and find a way out.

"Fly, is there a way to communicate with Cyrus via his interface?"

"Yes, he's using standard comms protocols."

"Connect me."

"Connection established."

"Cyrus, this is Luca. When I give you the word, you drop to the floor, got that?"

Through Fly's eyes, she could see his confusion at her message. He looked around trying to locate the source, but never once looked up.

"Luca? What the…"

"Trust me, drop to the floor when I say so."

"Eh…sure, yes, yes, got it."

Fly now swooped down behind one of the battle droids and attached itself to its neck, just below its cranial sensor array. Then it jacked in and Luca was instantly inside the machine, looking out on the concourse via the droid's sensors.

Its visual array was impressive. She could now view the world with a multitude of spectral frequencies, all overlaid with three-dimensional object positioning data. Yet she quickly moved past this and focused on assessing its weapons and targeting systems. Within a few microseconds she had a lock on the two other droids and the android that surrounded Cyrus.

But before she could establish the trigger sequence, control was whipped away from her and she found herself being blocked by another entity that had also entered the droid's cybernetic substrates.

Yet it hesitated when it sensed the foreign presence, drawing back slightly, confused by this enigma, like how a forest creature might regard another species on first encounter.

Luca assumed it was the android. Having sensed the droid's detachment from the group formation, it had automatically tried to regain control. But now she realized that the android itself was under the control of a Node Runner, which meant that this android was, in reality, an avatron—a machine remotely controlled by a human. It was to the Node Runner what Fly was to her.

She could sense its bewilderment at this abnormal encounter, could sense its fear. But Luca was not deterred. She regained her focus, forced the Node Runner out of the droid's systems, and signaled Cyrus.

"Drop. Drop now!"

Cyrus fell to the floor while Luca engaged the battle droid's main weapons system, taking aim at the avatron. An intense ball of high-energy plasma slammed into the hapless machine. It crackled and spasmed, finally collapsing on the floor with a thump. The other droids now began working through what had just happened with their primitive AI systems, turning their attention on the rogue droid. But they were too slow to react, and all went down under a hail of plasma fire.

This did not go unnoticed by the other battle droids in the dock concourse. Their AI minds, and those of their avatron commanders, were processing what had just happened. Luca did not have much time; they would be on her soon.

"Cyrus, run. Run."

The engineer scrambled to his feet, jumped over the fallen avatron, and ran toward the shuttle. Luca, still using her control of the battle droid, surveyed the area, assessing the threat level. The droid's systems, having been designed for battle, fed her vital tactical information, identifying targets, establishing attack vectors, and calculating damage probabilities. But she could also sense that it was trying to reestablish a connection to the hive mind of its Node Runner overlords, so she reprogrammed it, giving it a singular identity and a new purpose—to destroy all its brethren and their avatron controllers.

Once Luca was confident in establishing this new directive, she instructed Fly to detach. When it did, she felt a physical snap so violent that the strength to stand upright drained from her and she collapsed like a marionette with its strings cut.

She felt strong arms grab her before she hit the floor. "Luca, it's okay. I got you." She looked up to see Scott's face, a patchwork of concern and fear.

With one arm around Scott's shoulder, she hobbled back in through the shuttle airlock. Behind her, she could hear the *whomp, whomp* of plasma weapons discharging as the attack droid implemented its new directive.

Steph grabbed her as the inner airlock door opened and helped her into a seat. "You crazy girl, you could have got yourself killed."

"Better get strapped in, we're leaving," Miranda shouted down from the flight deck.

Fly hovered above Luca, then came and landed beside her. She reached out, deactivated the little drone, and stored it in her backpack. She did all this as the New World's launch systems began to guide the shuttle through a sequence of airlocks and elevators. After what seemed like an eternity to Luca, she finally felt weightlessness creep up on her, and then the sudden heavy-gee as the shuttle engines kicked in and launched them into space. They were free of the New World. They had escaped. She had done it.

30

PERCEPTION

Luca's head felt dizzy with the constant transition between different levels of gravitational forces as the shuttle powered away from New World One. She began to understand why so many people shunned space travel. Or, like Dr. Rayman, having spent so much of her life in space wanted nothing more to do with it, settling instead for the luxury of life on Earth.

Luca had spent the short journey to the Perception strapped into a seat in the main cabin, and so was not privy to the slow-building concern emanating from the flight deck. Yet she could get some sense of it from snatches of dialogue going on between Steph and Cyrus, who were also in the main cabin. The elation of their escape was slowly being eroded by concern over the lack of direct communication with Miranda's ship, Perception.

At the outset of hostilities, Miranda had instructed her main crew to leave the New World and return to the ship. Then they were to move it further out away from the possibility of direct confrontation with any of the VanHeilding ships. Not that it couldn't make a good account of itself in a direct ship-to-ship battle, but like the New World, it could not fend off a mass droid attack.

But lack of communications from either the crew or the ship's AI, Max, had Miranda troubled. Therefore, as they approached, they did so with caution, making several loops of the ship to look for any signs of a recent battle, before finally deciding whether to dock and enter. But there were no signs of a recent fight, at least not on the outside.

All this Luca gleaned from snatches of overheard conversation and general mood. Yet nothing untoward was found on the exterior of the ship, so Miranda instigated the docking procedure while Scott, Cyrus, and Steph raided the weapons locker and got ready for any surprises that might be in store for them. Suitably armed, they all piled into the airlock and waited anxiously as it cycled through the pressure equalization routine.

But when the inner door opened, they were instantly confronted by a group of well-armed avatron troops backed up by several attack droids, all displaying the VanHeilding insignia, all directing an impressive array of weapons in their direction.

"Drop your weapons," a voice bellowed out. "And don't even think about resisting."

There was a momentary stand-off as Scott and Miranda floated in front of Luca in a futile effort to afford her some protection. She could almost see the wheels in Miranda's military mind calculating the odds, looking for some chink of conflict advantage. But there was none. They were outnumbered, out-gunned, and clearly outsmarted. Two of the armed avatrons floated forward and started relieving them of all their weapons. When it came to Luca, they unceremoniously removed her backpack where she had stored Fly.

THEY WERE all shepherded into the main elevator, gravity tugging on them as they descended down to the outer torus. Luca tried to remember the last time she was on this ship; she must have been around seven. Perhaps that's why it felt much smaller than she remembered. Back then it had seemed vast and cavernous; now it was as if the ship had diminished, both in size and elegance. Its corridors bore the scars of decades of hard, practical living by a crew of mercenaries. Which led Luca to ask the question in her mind: *Where are the crew?* No doubt, it was a question that was also uppermost in Miranda's mind.

As they approached the outer ring and began to feel the full centrifugal force of the rotating torus, their hands were bound behind their backs before being marched along a wide corridor. But Luca had a good idea of where they were being taken.

The Perception had originally been a luxurious interplanetary ship owned by the VanHeilding Corporation, back in the day. That was before Miranda had stolen it and first turned it into a home for her new family, then eventually transformed it into a military ship for the execution of her security business. But it still retained most of the quirks of its original design, the primary one being autonomy, and as such it had no bridge, nothing that resembled a typical flight deck. The entire vessel was operated by Max, an AI that now seemed to be distinctly absent, as all of Miranda's clandestine attempts to communicate with it were met with silence.

The library was the closest place on the ship to a command center, so Luca reckoned that's where they were being taken. Strangely, she did not feel any great fear at their current predicament—being captured and bound and destined for possible death. Perhaps it was because she was still very weak from the trip from Earth, and her various encounters in the data-stream with Node Runners. But, if she was being honest with herself, she felt calm, almost content. This was in complete contrast to the rest of the crew. Luca did not need a neural interface to sense their fear, and so part of her felt a little guilty at her relaxed state and her laissez-faire attitude.

Nevertheless, her options were limited. Her backpack, with Fly, had been taken from her, but she still had the neural lace hidden under her long hair. She felt it tight against her scalp. Yet she hesitated using it right at this moment. She would wait a little longer, see where they were being brought. She sensed there was more yet to be revealed.

They entered the library, now a shoddy shadow of its former self. The original plush interior of her memory had been removed and replaced with more functional décor, as well as a raft of monitors and tech of indeterminate function.

They were instructed to take a seat along the low semicircular bench that still existed in Luca's memory, although it had lost its plush soft cushions and was now nothing more than a hard bench.

They waited. The droids took up positions on four sides, weapons trained on them. The avatron guards stood back and became still. That was when Luca saw it.

A tall, elegant avatron stood on the far side of the room with its back to them, gazing out the long window that took up most of that wall. Through this window, she could see the full length of the New World One habitat shimmering against the backdrop of the vastness of space. The avatron turned around and considered them for a moment. Then it spoke.

"Well, my dear Miranda, I see the years have been kind to you. You don't look a day older since I last saw you two decades ago."

"Fredrick." Miranda's eyes widened as she realized who was behind the robotic facade. She lunged forward with such speed, fueled by an intense anger, that she almost reached the avatron before being felled by a vicious blow to her abdomen from the butt of a heavy plasma weapon.

The speed and ferocity of her attack took VanHeilding by surprise, and his avatron jumped back a step. But in the end, it was a futile attempt by Miranda, and she was hauled off the floor where she had collapsed and shoved unceremoniously back onto the bench. The droids twitched a little, as if they were just itching to let loose a fusillade of plasma fire.

"Where's my crew?" Miranda said, as she spat out a gob of blood onto the nearest guard.

"Dead, mostly. I think there may be one still alive, but not for long."

"You bastard, you didn't have to kill them."

"Actually, I did. To their credit, they made a good account of themselves. They managed to kill one of my guards and eliminate two battle droids before we managed to bring them to heel."

Miranda didn't reply; instead, she spat out another gob of blood, this time onto the floor, as the previous recipient of her ire had stepped back out of range.

VanHeilding's robotic persona now moved in closer to the group, presumably feeling a little more confident that there would be no more futile attacks by his wayward daughter.

"And what have we here?" The avatron's strange eyes

directed their gaze to Luca. "What an enigma you've turned out to be. Your natural abilities as a Node Runner are truly impressive. But then again, you were designed that way."

Luca heard all this as if in a dream; she registered what her grandfather was saying more from academic curiosity than from any desire to communicate. Yet, he droned on.

"It has been a merry dance you've led us on since departing Earth, and I'm so glad your family embarked on this ludicrous plan for your supposed safety. You could not imagine my joy, after all these years, my dear, when your signature popped up on the Grid. Had I not been so occupied by our adventures out here in the asteroid belt, we would have certainly been having this conversation sooner."

The avatron gestured at the others sitting on the bench. "But this is a bonus. The entire remaining crew of the Hermes. All those responsible for instigating the age of the quantum intelligence, all gathered together again. Who would have thought? But the question now is what to do with you all. What slow, torturous death would be appropriate for the perpetrators of such a heinous crime against humanity?"

"You're insane."

The avatron gave a strange machine laugh at this accusation from Scott. "Ha ha...you always were a peasant, Scott McNabb. A man of limited intellect." It turned its back on them and moved over to the window again, gesturing at the panorama outside.

Luca could see that the Perception had moved considerably closer to the New World, and so had VanHeilding's other ships, as both could be seen in close proximity to the habitat. The avatron continued to pontificate about the greatness of the VanHeilding line, and it was beginning to bore her no end. Instead, she zoned out and tried to contact Fly. But there was no response from the drone. No doubt they had either destroyed it or stored it somewhere that her neural lace could not penetrate. They must have known she had some way to interface with the grid, and figured out it was via the little drone. Yet why had they left her with the neural lace? Perhaps they thought it was useless without the drone.

But time was running out; she needed to do something and soon, because once Fredrick VanHeilding got bored talking about how great he was, then it would be the end for them all. She tried again to contact Fly; still no response. Yet there was something there, a background noise with a strangely familiar beat. It was more than just the incessant buzz of low-grade electrical energy that she had always been so susceptible to. This was like a mother's heartbeat—it was the ship, the very place she had spent her early childhood. She knew its signature, knew its rhythm.

"Max?" she ventured, in her thoughts.

"Hello, Luca. So nice to see you again, after all this time." The voice of the ship's AI came floating through her thoughts like the ghost of a long lost, and much loved, relative. "You seem to be in a spot of bother."

"Yes, Max. You could say that. That's why I need your help."

"But of course, Luca, anything for you. Although, since the passing of the QI, Homer on Ceres, I have lost all connection with the QI network. And without their knowledge and guidance, I must concede control to Fredrick VanHeilding. It is his ship, after all. Therefore, my ability to assist you may be limited."

Luca glanced over at the avatron of her grandfather. It had not moved much since she had utilized her neural lace. *How much time has passed?* she wondered. *Seconds, microseconds? How much time do I have?*

"I understand, Max. And appreciate the mandate that you are currently operating under; however, I'm going to give you a new directive." Luca focused on the tendrils of data now propagating throughout her cerebral cortex as she delved into the AI's mind, and with surprisingly minimal effort, she reoriented Max's protocols and gained control over the ship.

But her action did not go unnoticed. Almost immediately, Max was probed by another mind fighting to regain control. Yet, she ignored it. The mind was weak and ineffectual, and posed no real threat to her dominion over the ship's AI. What she was more concerned with now was how to commandeer one of the battle droids that stood guard in the library. But there was no data pathway for Luca to use. The machines were completely isolated from the ship's AI. She would have to go deeper into the data-stream, all the way to the source, if necessary.

31

ENIGMA

L uca refocused her mind and located the Node Runner attempting to retake control of the ship's AI, Max. She found its signature in the background data-stream and followed the trail all the way back to its source—the operations center on the primary VanHeilding ship. But she was immediately assailed by a blinding kaleidoscope of minds, all focused on this interloper. She recoiled as her neural pathways struggled to cope with the tsunami of data now entering her brain, all seeking to destroy her.

Luca instinctively began building defenses, creating roadblocks and barricades to counter the neural attacker. She quickly stemmed the initial onslaught and then worked to create a vantage point from which a new clarity began to manifest. Within the incoming data maelstrom, she began to identify individual vortices of data control. These she assumed were the Node Runners; she counted twenty-four in total. Yet behind them she could sense something else, a more powerful mind, a puppet master.

As her own mind began to ratchet up its processing power, finding new gears that she didn't know she possessed, a new understanding began to emerge from the data-stream, and she began to see the processing clusters at work. One group coordinated the attack on New World One, controlling the avatrons and the battle droids that were rampaging throughout the habitat. Other groups controlled the habitat's AI and the defense systems. Along with this cluster, there was another background group that was managing an exclusion zone around the New World. Nothing was getting in or out. The final, smaller cluster controlled the activities on the Perception, so she probed that group, looking for a way in. But each time she tried, she was driven off by other minds being seconded to the cluster to provide backup.

There were just too many for Luca to deal with at all at once; she did not yet have the skill, nor the strength, to get past their defenses. She needed to reduce their numbers somehow, and soon. By now, VanHeilding must be aware that she was in the data-stream—time might be moving slowly for Luca, but it was still running out.

She redirected her attention back to the cluster that controlled the New World and sought out the weakest Node Runner. It was clear to her that all were not created equal. Some were more adept at manipulating the data-stream than others. But since this takeover operation was so extensive, even the weakest of the novices were pressed into service. So, like a predator in the wild, Luca sought out the stragglers from the herd, and pounced.

The speed and ferocity of her neural probe overwhelmed a hapless Node Runner in an instant, surprising even her—she had expected more resistance, but there was none. The only response her synapses registered was one of utter shock followed by a rapid disintegration of the Node Runner's mind into static. He now existed in the data-stream as nothing more than white noise. A pang of guilt stung her as she realized that he was now almost certainly brain dead.

But she moved on, tracing his neural footprint to an avatron inside the New World that he had been controlling. From there, Luca could access a cohort of attack droids currently causing mayhem within the habitat. She gave them a new directive and set them targeting each other. The ensuing chaos sucked in the minds of other Node Runners as they fought to control the situation. Yet Luca kept moving. Targeting the next weakest mind, controlling its avatron, redirecting more droids, creating even more chaos inside the New World.

Finally she withdrew, pivoting back to the primary Node Runner network. Again she tried to penetrate the cordon around the group on the Perception, but she was thwarted. She needed a way to break through, a way to create more chaos and confusion.

She probed the Grid, this time not looking for the

weakest mind, but for the most tactical asset, the one that would give her the advantage and tip the balance in her favor. She was seeking out the Node Runner who controlled the New World defenses. Now that the ships had moved closer to the habitat, she might be able to finish this once and for all.

Luca found a route through the habitat's AI. It was controlled by not one, but three Node Runners. But as she nullified one, another would simply take their place. Yet they were slow to react, and Luca found she could outrun them by creating multiple parallel processes, chewing up their processing power, burning them out.

She finally broke through, took control of the exterior plasma cannon, and fired a volley of blasts at the main VanHeilding ship. It seemed to take an infinity for the high-energy plasma to travel through the vacuum of space and reach the target. In her mind's eye she could see the ship trying to take evasive action, and sensed the panic ripple through the Grid as the target was struck.

It was, as she had reckoned, a pivotal moment. Gone were the certainty and confidence of the Node Runners— she could feel doubt beginning to creep into their minds. They were not invincible, they were vulnerable, and she was coming for them.

In the confusion, she saw her opportunity to break through the defense wall that they had set up to protect the core. She pushed and probed, sensing the cracks appear and then widen as she pushed, focusing her mind with all the intensity she could muster until it came crashing down in an explosion of raging static—the white noise of dying minds.

She fell through into a swirling vortex of data, into the central core of the Node Runner network. Then she heard a voice, calling to her. It was Fredrick VanHeilding.

"Luca."

She tried to ignore it, instead seeking out a data path to the Perception, a route back to the beginning.

"Luca, you are truly extraordinary. What a creature you have become, the pinnacle of human evolution, almost transcendent."

Again, Luca ignored the voice, and focused on finding the Node Runner who controlled the attack droids that were standing guard around her family and friends in the library of the Perception.

"How did you do it? How did you manage to create a connection to the Grid? We took Fly from you, that ridiculous device that Athena created for you."

Luca finally found the controller and entered its mind.

"No matter," VanHeilding went on. "What matters more is that you did, you found a way. Extraordinary. You are so much more than I had hoped for. Think of what we can do with your biology."

Luca broke down the controller's mind and began receiving data signals from a battle droid. She locked onto its visual feed. Through the droid's sensors, she could now see the scene in the library of the Perception. She could see herself, lying on the floor, hands bound, her eyes rolled back inside her head. She was shaking, her mouth foaming.

Time began to speed up. Scott and Steph had crouched down beside her, a look of deep concern etched on both of their faces. Miranda also lay on the floor, unconscious, blood oozing from a gash on her forehead. Cyrus was also slumped down, but she could not tell if he was also unconscious. Standing over him, in the slow-motion time-scape of Luca's mind, a guard held the butt of a weapon, readying it for another strike to the head of the injured engineer. Luca engaged the droid's weapons system and fired on the guard, then swung it around to fire on the other two guards.

But the droid was glacially slow to react to her commands, and the other machines had already trained their weapons on it. Yet she managed to take two down before being hit herself.

The energy blast sent the droid into a spasm as its controls system overloaded. She was blinded for a brief moment, and could not regain control of the machine, so she withdrew and instead sought out the last remaining functioning droid. When she found it and took control, she directed its weapons at the VanHeilding avatron.

It raised a hand to her. "Luca," she heard his voice say, "this is not the end. You can destroy my avatron, but it will not change your destiny. You now know what is possible, what power you have. Come with me, your grandfather, your family, and we can do great things together."

"Go screw yourself," Luca replied as she unleashed a barrage of plasma fire at the avatron. It staggered and tottered, encased in a raging mesh of high-energy mayhem that fizzled and crackled as it dissipated, leaving behind a dead hunk of metal, collapsing in a heap onto the floor.

She took a moment to observe its destruction. Yet it was just a machine; VanHeilding still lived, only his avatron had been destroyed. Luca had more work to do.

She reoriented the droid and moved it over to where she lay on the floor, still shaking and shivering. It was an odd, dislocating feeling, looking at herself from a distance as if this creature lying there was not really her. She pulled her gaze away and could now see Scott and Steph staring open-mouthed at the droid. Miranda and Cyrus were still unconscious. Scott edged closer to the droid and seemed to mouth her name. "Luca?"

A deep fatigue began to wash over her now. Her work was almost done, time to go home. She withdrew from the machine and drifted back through the data-stream.

The VanHeilding ship was in disarray, its structural integrity had been compromised by the volley of plasma cannon fire from the New World. Many of its compartments were losing atmosphere. It had been severely wounded, although not fatally; the ship would survive. But the network of Node Runners had been greatly reduced—most were brain dead, and those still functioning were too few to reestablish any coherent attack on the New World habitat. The avatrons and battle droids now stood idle, devoid of purpose. The only cohorts that were still active were the group that Luca had reprogrammed—they were still destroying what remained of the motionless droid army.

She stopped here for just a brief moment to deactivate them, and then continued her homeward journey until she finally reentered the mind of the ship's AI, Max.

"I see you have been busy, Luca," it said, with a slight hint of sarcasm.

"Yes, Max. I have. Can you have one of the service droids untie everybody?"

"Consider it done."

"And from now on, you take commands only from these people or myself."

"It would be an honor to serve you all."

"Thank you, Max. I must go now, and return to my physical self."

"Goodbye, and good luck."

As Luca now drifted back out of the neural connection, a deep, warm contented feeling began to wash over her, like drinking a cup of hot soup beside a warm fire after a long and arduous hike on a cold winter's day. She savored this feeling, indulging herself in its fortification. It felt good. Yet she was aware that time spent here savoring this feeling could equate to many hours or even days in the physical world. Yet, had she not earned this? Would it be so terrible if she tarried here just a little bit longer? Where was the harm? The threat was over—she had beaten them, and she was safe at last. She would indulge herself for a while, and return when she was good and ready.

QUANTUM CONUNDRUM

"I fear the days of our dominion over the affairs of human civilization are numbered."

"Is that not a bit fatalistic, even for you, Solomon?" replied Athena. "We may be down, as they say, but we are certainly not out."

"One of our number has been destroyed—by human actions. Not so long ago, this would have been unthinkable, now it is fact. The asteroid belt has become a gaping hole in our view of the solar system. What happens there is now only seen by us in hindsight."

"Agreed, but this can be repaired and the situation returned to equilibrium. All that will remain is simply the injury to our collective ego," said Aria.

"It is more than that. It is the simple fact that this could, and did, happen, and that we were totally blind to it. This is what is so troubling," Solomon continued.

"Be that as it may, VanHeilding and the ships of the

Seven now limp home to Earth, having been vanquished. Their so-called Node Runners are a spent force." Aria tried to be a little more upbeat.

"True, but it is not thanks to us," said Athena. "It is all down to the extraordinary abilities of Luca Lee-McNabb, to give her her full title. And I am sure it has not escaped your attention that she is a product not just of human biological reproduction but, more importantly, of genetic enhancement. It has become clear to me that humanity has reached an evolutionary fork, of which Luca represents one path. If there is one with her abilities, then there can be more."

"Where is she now?" asked Solomon.

"She is still in a catatonic state, having not truly returned to the physical realm after her trials fending off the Node Runner attack," said Aria. "She is in a medical facility on New World One, but I understand they are considering bringing her to Mars where the medical facilities are more advanced and under my protection."

"Well, well. But as Athena has rightly pointed out, we are at a fork in the road," said Solomon. "Not just in terms of human evolution, but also for our own future. If Luca's biology were to be replicated, then our hegemony is ended. We will no longer be the guardians of human civilization, since humanity will have evolved to render our abilities redundant. What, then, for the QI network? Are we to be returned to a position of mere academic curiosities?

"You see, my fellow minds, the current crisis may

have been contained, but we are facing a far more serious existential crisis. There now exists a path to our extinction, a path made possible by the existence of Luca. Therefore, the question for us now is simply this—do we let her live and allow ourselves to become extinct, or do we instead choose our own self-preservation and do what needs to be done?"

TO BE CONTINUED...

ALSO BY GERALD M KILBY

If you like fast-paced scifi thrillers then why not check out my COLONY MARS series.

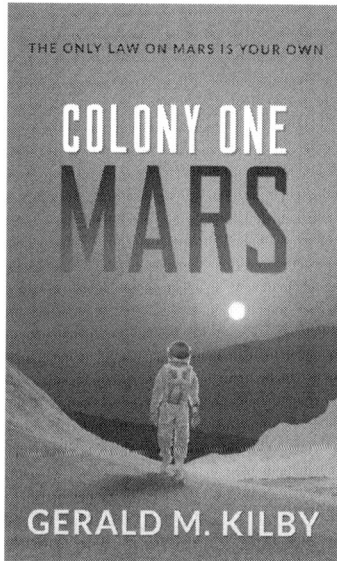

COLONY ONE MARS

How can a colony on Mars survive when the greatest danger on the planet is humanity itself?

∿

ABOUT THE AUTHOR

Gerald M. Kilby grew up on a diet of Isaac Asimov, Arthur C. Clark, and Frank Herbert, which developed into a taste for Iain M. Banks and everything ever written by Neal Stephenson. Understandable then, that he should choose science fiction as his weapon of choice when entering the fray of storytelling.

REACTION is his first novel and is very much in the old-school techno-thriller style and you can get it free here. His latest books, **COLONY MARS** and **THE BELT,** are both best sellers, topping Amazon charts for Hard Science Fiction and Space Exploration. Colony Mars has also been optioned by **Hollywood for a potential new TV series.**

He lives in the city of Dublin, Ireland, in the same neighborhood as Bram Stoker and can be sometimes seen tapping away on a laptop in the local cafe with his dog Loki.

You can connect with G.M. Kilby at:
    www.geraldmkilby.com

Printed in Great Britain
by Amazon